One Two

One Two
Eliane Brum

Translated by
Lucy Greaves

amazoncrossing

Text copyright © 2012 Eliane Brum
Translation copyright © 2014 Lucy Greaves

Previously published as *Uma Duas* by Leya Brazil in 2012. Translated from Brazilian Portuguese by Lucy Greaves.

Published by AmazonCrossing, Seattle
www.apub.com

Amazon, the Amazon logo, and AmazonCrossing are trademarks of Amazon.com, Inc., or its affiliates.

ISBN-13: 9781477819531
ISBN-10: 1477819533

Cover design by David Drummond, Salamander Hill Design
Library of Congress Control Number: 2013919543
Printed in the United States of America

For João

01

My arm's laughter. Blood oozing from my arm's mouth. How many times have I cut myself?

And my mother's voice on the other side of the door. Laura. I tear another mouth. My blood drips onto the bedroom floor, together with the voice. Laura. My mother has always been like this. She always knows what I'm doing.

I'm starting to write this book while my mother tries to break the door down with her old woman's fingernails. Because this reality is too real. I need a chance. I want a chance. So does she.

As I type the first word, blood still stains the teeth of my arm's mouth. Of all my arm's mouths. I don't cut myself again after the first word. Now I'm fiction. As fiction, I can exist.

This is the story. And this is how it happened. At least for me.

02

Your metaphors are a heap of shit! the boss yells at her, out-
raged by the metaphor she's placed on the sheet of paper.

She looks at him, her eyes wide with hurt. She sees that
he has a blue tail. Blue and phosphorescent. And it's not meta-
phorical. It's a real, reptilian tail. Viscous and slippery. There, a
string of adjectives for the boss's lack of noun. Disgust blocks
her throat and at that same moment she hears the siren.
Insistent. They've found out that the boss is a blue lizard. She
feels pleasure in the form of sweet vomit. The siren is getting
louder all the time. She wakes up.

The phone is ringing on the bedside table she inherited
from the grandmother she never met. What time is it? Light is
coming in through the slits in the blind. The clock shows 8:43
a.m. She answers. A woman's voice on the other end. Who's
that? She hates it when people call and ask her to identify herself. There's nothing worse. Who do you want? she replies. The
voice snorts. Or the voice's breath does. Is this Maria Lúcia's
daughter? That's not how she normally chooses to introduce
herself. But it is her. You need to come to your mother's apartment right now. Who's this crazy woman waking her up to
give her orders over the phone? Sorry, can you say that again?
Your mother's not well, we can't open the door. Who are you?

I'm Alzira, from the spiritualist center. Are you at my mother's apartment? I came here because we hadn't seen Maria Lúcia for a while and we were worried, but I can't get in. Your mother won't open the door. She can't open it. The building manager has called the fire department, but it'll be quicker if you've got a key. And, anyway, we think you should be here. You're her only daughter. Her brain stubbornly retains the blue image of the lizard boss, but reality shakes her with a greater insanity. She can get her head around a boss with a tail, but not this phone call. I'll be right there, she says. She drops the phone. It hangs there like a hangman. A hangwoman. She'd like to hang Alzira-from-the-spiritualist-center for crashing in with her inescapable reality. Couldn't it be the other way around? Couldn't the lizard boss be real, and the mother stuck in her apartment a nightmare she could always wake up from with the light coming in through the slits in the blind? Shitty life, shitty mother, shitty woman-from-the-spiritualist-center. Shitty people sticking their noses into other people's lives. What's Alzira doing at her mother's, anyway? And how did she get this number? Where's the shitty goddamn key to her mother's apartment? She's had that key for ages but never used it because she always rings the bell when she goes to her mother's place. She doesn't want any surprises when she goes to her mother's apartment. She remembers her mother giving her the key for emergencies or in case she needed to drop by one day. And she remembers saying she didn't want the key, she didn't want any key that would take her inside her mother. In the end, she begrudgingly put the key in her pocket, ignoring her mother's feigned hurt, and later she threw it into a corner, but where? She tips out the bedside table drawer, spilling its contents onto the bed. Condoms, probably expired, a red lipstick, really red, but broken, that silver earring she thought she'd lost, a ticket for a play she loved, a man on the parapet of a bridge, a woman, a stale chocolate bonbon, trash trash trash. And no key. She wants to tell nosy-Alzira-from-the-spiritualist-center that, no, she doesn't have a key, she doesn't give a shit about the door her mother won't or can't open, and she has things to do, she has to work and get on with her own life instead of worrying about her crazy mother, who clings to life when she doesn't want her anymore, who pretends it's not too late for the two of them. But goddamn-nosy-Alzira-from-the-spiritualist-center didn't leave a number, and she refused the offer of caller ID because she thinks they've no right to charge for something that should be free.

She doesn't shower. She gets dressed in last night's ciga-rette-scented clothes, puts on some nude lipstick but doesn't brush her teeth. She hails a taxi on the corner and gives the driver her mother's address. Now that the blue-tailed boss is just a memory from another life, she feels a tightness in her stomach. She's angry at her mother and scared for her mother. This mother who stubbornly goes on being real. More alive still because she hates her mother just as intensely as she loves her, even though she tries to only hate her. What's her mother playing at now? What's all this about not opening the door? If she's playing the victim, she won't go and see her at Christmas. She wants to scratch her mother with her nails until she sees her bleed, she wants to break a nail on one of her mother's bones. And then comes the remorse, the god-damn remorse that always hits her like a kind of stomachache. Her gastritis has a first name and a surname and was once called womb.

The driver forgot to start the meter. That old trick. She hands him a twenty-real note and doesn't wait for change. Her mother's house is nearby, after all. Too near and too far. She's startled. What's going on up ahead? Are they filming one of those sensationalist TV shows? Firemen, military police, an ambulance. Where's the helicopter? If her mother isn't dead, she's going to kill her for making such a scene, showing her up as she sneaks around the edges of the small, ordered world she's managed to build in spite of her mother. The old doorman is waiting for her at the entrance, looking worried. Everyone's there, they're going to break the door down. She runs up the six flights of stairs. Her heart is pounding from exhaustion and all these unwelcome feelings. She has to start going to the gym again if she wants to be able to climb stairs once she turns forty. There's a crowd in the hall that her mother shares with a neighbor. What's going on? she asks. Everyone looks at her. I'm her daughter. And they don't like her confession or that witness for the prosecution look of hers. What do they know about her, anyway? They've been tricked by that arsenic-smooth old woman.

How long is it since you last saw her?

What kind of question is that? I think I spoke to my mother on the phone three or four weeks ago, maybe more. You think? They flash looks of mutual understanding, then pretend she isn't there. She hates looks of mutual understanding. Now she's the ungrateful daughter. They've already condemned her, and now they're ignoring her. Maria Lúcia, shouts the one who by now is accusing-nosy-Alzira-from-the-spiritualist-center, her mouth almost stuck to the door. She hears the gasping on the other side almost like a silence. She doesn't recognize that voice as her mother's, it can't be her mother's, but it is. Laura, is that you? Goddamn mother, showing her up like this, revealing her to the goddamn world that knows nothing of what her mother did to her. And she hears the door giving way to the strength of the young fireman's biceps and triceps, the fireman who'll never consider fucking her because he's disgusted by her because she's a bitch who doesn't know how long it's been since she last spoke to her mother. How would he know that she isn't a bitch at all, that she doesn't want to be a daughter and her mother doesn't want to be a mother, and, anyway, why should she care what this cliché of a fireman thinks? Why does every fireman have to be a cliché? Are they already clichés before they become firemen, or do they become clichés in order to become firemen? The sound is now an explosion and she feels her bones sticking to the peeling gray wall. Mold finds its way in through her nose and clutches at her lungs with claws she knows she can't escape.

The open door. It takes her a while to understand the open door. Where's her mother? She can't see her. A barely perceptible touch on her right shin. Her mother. The flesh curled up on the floor is her mother. When the realization reaches her like one of those bullets that shatters into millions of pieces on impact, she screams. For a moment, she's at the bottom of a swimming pool, shouting silently while the water fills her lungs and carries her to a place free of suffering. And her mother grabs her hair and pulls her back up to the surface because she won't let her leave. Now the pain's burning her lungs and the salt of her tears is mixing with the chlorine running from her eyes. She's there again, on the surface, gasping for breath in the most complete silence, because words never measured up to her pain so she doesn't even bother searching for them. This time, however, it's her voice that screams when she sees the flesh curled at her feet. Finally, the scream that's been trapped inside her is released. And she feels like the scream will never end, the scream is forevermore, it's a scream for all of life and beyond life. Because now she faces horror in its entirety. And screams are things that don't become words, words that can't be said. There's no way to escape a mother's flesh. The womb is forever.

03

———

That's not how I wanted to write. Books were always the window through which I escaped this mother who, now, as I write with blood trickling, is listening at the door. When I open a book, I disappear. It's been like that ever since I was a girl. I don't mean that metaphorically. Maybe the lizard-tail boss is right. I can't write metaphors because I don't understand them. I take everything literally. Like my arms, embroidered with the scars of all the attempts to separate myself from my mother's body. I never had an umbilical cord that could be cut. Just the pain of being confused with my mother's body, of being my mother's flesh. This ritual that now drips off me like a failure. Another one. I cut cut cut and still don't know if I exist. I still don't have a body. And she's there outside, scared I might leave, pretending not to know that I can't leave. I never could. Because I drag her body with me. It engulfs me and swallows me.

But I'm rambling.

I was always scared of writing. Of making my blood a symbol for blood. I was scared of the unfamiliar pain that might come, a certainty that I could almost touch. Although the blood I bleed is real, I know this ritual. It is the little I have. It's a constitution. I constitute myself through my cuts. No, not through words. What will they do to me?

Will words kill me? Is there life after words? That question is a blanket of fear that wraps around me while my mother presses her ear to the door. Or is there life without blood? I'm waging everything on this now. I write in the hope that words will free me from blood. From my mother's body. But what if I don't exist beyond this mixture of mother flesh and daughter flesh? I feel myself slip through the black hole of her body, where I am blind and my knife slashes the air.

I can hear her labored breathing behind the door. I know she wants me to hear her. Does she know I'm killing her? Not like the other times, but definitively? A death beyond death?

But I'm rambling.

I'm troubled now by something less dense. I don't write as I'd like to. The phrases that emerge from me are worthless. Do they contain some truth, at least? If I'm nothing but this tortured body that is an extension, not a possession, what can I say that is mine? Words crawl out of me like fat bloody worms, and I suspect there's no subject saying, There's no me. So, who is speaking? Whose are the words that constrain me?

I hear her breath scratching at the door. And I'm scared. But I carry on.

04

————

Alzira shakes her like a rag doll. I've got so much flesh, woman-of-the-spirits, too much flesh. Alzira seems to want to slap her like they do in the soaps she watches every night before and after speaking with the dead, she's scared and needs to blame someone. But something Alzira sees in her gaze makes her hand stop before it hits her face. She doesn't know yet if the scream escaped or simply echoed inside her. Alzira carries on shaking her. Stop, she says. Stop. I'm fine.

She notices the smell. And remembers her mother bundled up at her feet. Her mother is no longer there. She's been put on a stretcher that appeared out of nowhere. She should be able to describe the smell, but she can't. Her mother's been dead for days, she thinks. Then her mother says, Laura. It's a new voice. What did you do, Mom? There's a hate that she doesn't want her voice to betray. Laura, says her mother again.

Are you coming? asks Alzira. Am I going? Yes, I think I am. She goes downstairs behind the stretcher, which doesn't fit in the elevator. Are you a relative? asks the paramedic. She mumbles that, yes, she's her daughter. How did your mother end up like this? She doesn't answer. Do you live in another city? She doesn't answer. She knows he's judging her too. That she's the one guilty of letting her mother rot alive in her apartment. Blame the distant daughter. The indifferent daughter. The ungrateful daughter. How could they know that there's no distance between them? That for them, no separation is possible? That when the mother began to rot in her apartment, something in the daughter started to smell? That it wasn't the mother's suicide, but the daughter's murder?

Her face is a mask as she answers the social worker's questions. A talking mask. No, she didn't know that her mother couldn't walk anymore. No, she didn't know that they cut the electricity off more than a month ago because the bill hadn't been paid. No, she didn't know that her mother hadn't eaten for over a week. No, she didn't know that the cat had eaten part of her mother's foot. No, she didn't know. Why didn't she know? Because her mother didn't tell her. Because she works Monday to Monday. Because the two of them aren't close. No, they aren't close, because they're the same person, she almost says. Yes, she does have a private health plan, but her mother never wanted to be her dependent. Because she likes her daughter to be dependent on her. She doesn't give this last answer either.

The social worker tries hard to forge her own mask to cover the repulsion she feels for the daughter, but she isn't all that good at it. You're going to have to juggle things to take care of your mother. Do you think you can manage? Yes, she can manage. No, she doesn't want to. No, she doesn't have a choice.

She walks through corridors that stink of state healthcare. There must be some law that requires public hospitals to have peeling walls and broken chairs, she thinks. A persistent kind of decay that smells of death, formaldehyde, and cheap scent. The smell of cheap scent moves her. That try-hard scent has an intangible dignity that rips at the spongy flesh inside her nose and makes her eyes well up. Cheap scent saves the world every day, she knows that now.

She finds Alzira in the ICU waiting room. Alzira thinks she's crying over her mother, not the cheap scent. You mother has a strong heart, Alzira says. I know. We knew something was up, your mother looked skinnier every time she came to meetings. But, you know, your mother was always a very reserved woman. Yes, her mother must have hidden the horror of her condition from them. Do you have enough money for everything? Yes, she has money. So does her mother. She has no idea why her mother didn't pay the electricity bill or why she wasn't eating. Her mother always refused to get a maid because she's fiercely protective of her privacy. She always hated the idea of anyone else touching her things, she was always so orderly. Her mother worries that someone might discover the bodies neatly folded in her drawers, she almost says.

She regrets telling Alzira too much, she stops talking. She doesn't want her to think she's apologizing, because she isn't. She frowns. She says she's going back to the apartment to get what they need and turns away. Laura, says her mother's new voice. She turns, but only Alzira's spirit-spotting gaze meets hers. No, Alzira, the dead aren't the ones to fear. The living are. Oh, Alzira, if you could see the living, you wouldn't have such well-being stamped triumphantly across your face.

05

She interrupts the taxi driver as soon as he starts moaning about the traffic. They found my mother rotting in her apartment. The man doesn't know if it's a joke or if his passenger is crazy. She congratulates herself. She's managed to get a taxi driver to shut up. When she gets to the building, everything seems normal. This is what always scares her about the world, that way hell has of hiding in the light. Not in the shadows, as the authors of horror stories would have us believe. An old man is sunbathing, two neighbors talk while their dogs shit in quivering synchronicity. Only the doorman watches her shyly, showing a glimmer of solidarity. The first she's seen. I thought about calling you, but the building manager said we shouldn't stick our noses in. You know, the people who live here like their privacy. Yes, she knows. It's one of the things she likes about that building. Everyone seems to know everyone else's business, and, generally speaking, they do know. But no one asks anything. Not directly, at least.

She takes the elevator up this time. The service one, so she won't bump into anybody. She shares the small space with a trash can and a janitor, but he doesn't say a word. It's good when a person's position prevents him or her from asking questions. Marx's class war isn't actually a war, it's just a division between those who may ask questions and those who are only authorized to give answers.

The door is unlocked but she automatically shoves a hand into her pocket all the same, only to discover that the keys to her mother's flat were there all along. Her unconscious is clever. It knew she'd run inside when necessary, ready to drown in her mother's body.

Now the door is wide open. A battered door, bearing marks that will never be removed. She feels sorry for the door as she strokes the wounds made by forceps. A second later, the smell reaches her nose and urges her to vomit. She starts running toward the bathroom but discovers midway that it's useless. She throws up right there, her guts mixed with her mother's. Shit, snot, vomit, and who knows what else on the floor. How could her mother do it? Her shoes poke into her mother.

No, she can't do that by herself. She takes off her coat, rolls it up in her hand, and grabs the dirty intercom. I need a good house cleaner. No, not one, two. Do you know anyone? I'll pay double. And I need a locksmith. The old doorman knows someone. He knows a lot of people who can clean up any mess. People who every day have to clean up other people's shit so it doesn't leave a stain. She sits at the top of the stairs to wait. She hears a meow that adheres to her eardrums and makes the hairs on her arms stand on end. The cat, she remembers. That goddamn fat cat her mother treated like a beloved son. The incestuous hairball ate part of her mother's foot. Great job. Now the meow sounds like a roar. And she's scared. She thinks about going down to get the doorman, but she knows it's her job to sort it out. She creeps into the apartment, looking for a piece of wood or metal, something she can use to hit the cat and turn it into just another smudge of organic matter on the floor. With another roar, the cat jumps onto her face, suffocating her, its claws grabbing onto the back of her head and neck, digging into her flesh. She feels the monster inside her responding to the monster outside. And she likes it.

She plunges her nails into the cat, and, for a moment, the two of them dance a clumsy ballet. The cat clings to her face like the creature from Alien. She feels her nails driving deep into the animal's flesh. She can't see, but she knows the cat doesn't stand a chance in this test of strength. The creature breaks under her nails. Then it's no longer suffocating her, but she likes the feeling of her fingers playing with its entrails. Is that a kidney? A lung? She pulls the warm, now limp body away from her face. The animal is still breathing, and she sees the hate in its bloodshot eyes. The miserable beast is dying and still isn't scared of her. There's a strand of her red hair caught in its broken claws. It's so thin, she thinks. That's it, cannibal. You don't need to sleep with my mother anymore. And with that, she pulls the cat apart. She throws it onto the floor, next to the rest.

Two women are watching her from the doorway, in shock. The cat, she says. It attacked me. I had to kill it. It ate part of my mother's foot. The women nod silently. I'm going to wash my hands. She pushes aside a pile of dishes that must have been there for weeks, maybe months, and turns on the tap. A mixture of the cat's blood and her own runs down the crockery that once belonged to her mother's mother. Throw everything out, we're going to have to buy new plates. She dries her hands on her trousers. Your hair, says one of the women. She follows her gaze with her left hand. Blood and something else. It might need stitches. Maybe you should go to the emergency room, ma'am. Yes, I will. But first, I want to talk you through the cleaning. Throw everything out. The crockery, the bedsheets, the towels, anything you find on the floor. Use a hose to wash

everything down, even the ceiling and the walls. Then disinfect everything with ammonia. Every last thing. We can't start
until tomorrow. Today we're cleaning a place on the tenth floor.
Tomorrow, then. The locksmith will be here soon to replace the
lock. Pick up the key from the doorman tomorrow. I'll come
by at the end of the day and settle up with you. It's going to
take two days. Maybe three. Then ask the doorman to call me
when you've finished. He's got my number. What about the
cat? Throw the cat in the trash. I don't think we can do that, the
younger woman says. It's a body. Do something with it, then.
I'll pay extra for that. Bury it, burn it, whatever. Are you really
going to pay us double? the older woman asks. Yes, double.
But I want it left as if nothing ever happened here. I don't want
there to be any smell, any trace, anything. Like nothing happened. We understand. The two women turn away. Are they
mother and daughter, the mother instructing her daughter how
to make clean people's filth disappear? The older one pauses
before walking into the elevator. She seems to want to ask
something. Then she remembers that she belongs to the class
of people who don't ask questions. And in she goes.

　　The cat looks like a slipper on the floor. Stained red. She
feels sorry for it. Another one of her mother's victims. Or hers?
Collateral damage. The scene scrolls through her mind, the
cat that used to sleep on her mother's bed, purring beside her
mother's belly, starts to eat her foot after it's gone hungry for
two days. While it was chewing her big toe, did she call it my
love? My life? Would she eat her mother if she was hungry, if
she hadn't eaten for two days and was stuck in the apartment?
She doesn't feel the vomit coming. She just throws up. Again.
Nothing but bile, because she remembers now that she hasn't
eaten since last night. She wipes her mouth on her forearm,
because everything about her stinks of blood or guts or spit

or other unidentifiable things. She doesn't worry about closing the door. No one would be brave enough to go in there, the smell hits you out in the corridor. She goes downstairs. The smell follows her, because she's rotting too. Since when?

She leaves the money for the locksmith with the doorman, who looks at her pityingly. She hates being pitied, but it's such an unusual occurrence that she fails to feel angry. She leaves a tip for everything as well. Especially for not asking. And she walks to the corner, where all the taxis ignore her. She must look terrible with her bleeding face and dirty clothes, and does she have crazy eyes? Just then she remembers that she ought to tell the blue-tailed boss. She rummages in her bag for her cell phone. Sorry for not calling earlier, but my mother had a heart attack. No, no, she's fine now, but I'm going to have to stay at the hospital. I'll stop by tomorrow and sort everything out. No, no, I don't need anything. It's all under control. She hangs up and for a moment sees herself from above, on the corner, a woman who's still young but whose face looks like it has weathered millennia, her long red hair flowing like blood, out of place on her ashen body. And, yes, everything is under control. It always was. Aren't they all good at pretending? All those who blame her, not for her current state but because her misery exposes them? Don't you worry, she wants to scream at all of them. My tragedy isn't going to denounce anyone. I just need to get home and have a bath. And then we'll all be safe again.

An old taxi stops. Do you need a ride, young lady? Yes, she does. She gets into the grubby backseat, which doesn't smell much better than she does. She gives the address. If you don't mind, ma'am, could you put the seat belt on? You know, ma'am, the police are already on my back about the state of the car, never mind passengers without seat belts. I do mind, actually, she says. Excuse me? He doesn't understand. Do I look like I need a seat belt? He says nothing then. Did you fall? Yes. I tripped and fell down the stairs in my mother's building. Do you want me to take you to the emergency room? No, it's fine. I just need a shower. It looks like you've got some pretty bad cuts there, ma'am. She smiles. Now it is a crazy person's smile. I'm used to taking care of cuts. She did it again. The driver falls silent. For the rest of the journey, this time.

Her face in the bathroom mirror looks worse than she thought. Much worse. She looks like Linda Blair after she was possessed. Her hair is like a rat's nest. She remembers the cat and thinks it's funny that a rat's nest came to mind. She slowly peels off her clothes and gets into the shower. She clenches her teeth when the water hits her cuts. This is a familiar, almost pleasurable pain. Now she knows where she is. She washes the cuts with plenty of soap. Then she looks in the bathroom cabinet for a sterile needle and thread, and neatly stitches her face and neck. Just a few more scars, visible ones this time. She applies a layer of antiseptic cream and swallows two anti-inflammatories while the bathtub fills. She opens a tin of condensed milk, pours it out into a large bowl, and grabs a tablespoon. She sinks into the hot water. She turns on the jets, and the familiar sound of the motor covers all other noises. Soon, she'll be inside a womb that does her no harm. Closing her eyes tight, she starts to lick the sweet milk.

06

She wakes up to Cat Stevens. Where do the children play? She lets the alarm clock play through to the end of the song. She wants to hear it again, then she remembers. She's shocked by the sun coming in through the slits in the blind. It always shocks her. It's true that the dinosaur is still there, but how can life admit such horror and carry on regardless? She wants to become catatonic because it would be good not to suffer, but she's not like that. She does suffer. Her muscles are painfully stiff from the day before, but she's almost happy. It's as if all that stuff happened so long ago that it didn't even happen to her. Is it true that yesterday she found her mother rotting alive in her own shit? And that she killed her mother's cat with her bare hands, ripping it in half? The cat that ate part of her mother's foot? In some strange way, as with everything they've previously gone through, she's able to assimilate it and even feel wearily pleased with this sunny morning.

Her mother in the ICU. She's gripped by a sudden sense of urgency. Annoyance. Guilt. She needs to check whether her mother is alive or dead. Suddenly the thought of her mother dying seems unbearable. Sitting in bed, she bursts out crying. She cries so much that the pillow gets damp and sticky. Her sobs get gradually further apart, and she's exhausted again.

She gets under the shower and carefully washes her long atheist-believer's hair, the one dissonant note in her effort to go unnoticed.

She's in a taxi again, with her hair in a ponytail, under control. Yes, life is under control. No, she doesn't like politics. Yes, she agrees that all politicians are thieves. No, she doesn't think the dictatorship was better. She so desperately wants to have a normal conversation that she enthusiastically quotes Churchill: "Democracy is the worst form of government except all the others that have been tried." No, the driver doesn't know who Winston is. Even so, he's shocked. Enough to change the subject. Are you going to visit a relative? Yes, my mother. She had a heart attack yesterday. She's in the ICU. And she feels compelled to explain. I wanted to stay at the hospital last night, but they don't let you. The taxi driver starts railing against the public health system. And he tells the story of an aunt who had to wait six months for chemotherapy while cancer was eating her from the inside out.

She wanders the corridors with their flaking paint and broken chairs, which now smell of formaldehyde, death, cheap scent, and something else. Disinfectant. Morning in the hospital, windows are opened to chase away the night's dead. People tend to die at dawn, apparently, something to do with a hormone. She read that somewhere. The good thing about the ICU is that they don't expect you to visit. They're almost glad when there are no questions from relatives. There are lots of beds with intubated patients attached to all kinds of wires, and only a few professionals to ensure that they aren't scared, or screaming. The silence is satisfying, interrupted only by the regular purr of machines. Here, death is almost an abstraction. It's all under control if you manage to ignore the terrified eyes of those who can't move or speak. I'd like to know how Maria

Lúcia Siqueira is, please. She was brought in yesterday. The woman in white's knowing look contains something else. No, her mother isn't a normal patient. In here, she can't pretend it was a heart attack. Her mother, of course, wouldn't tolerate anything so civilized. She's stable, but her kidney function isn't good. She might need dialysis. And she's very dehydrated. She can almost feel the accusation in the nurse's voice. But the nurse is worn out from her shift and the misfortunes that fill her days and doesn't have the strength to sustain her indignation for more than a few seconds. The nurse wants to go home and sleep. Just sleep. The nurse must need sunny mornings too.

Do you want to speak to your mother? It's visiting hours now. Can I? I think you ought to.

The nurse's mouth twists into a expression of resentment. That's it, the nurse got her revenge on someone. She can go home with her fake Louis Vuitton bag, feeling superior. I'll go and see her, then. Five minutes, OK? Is there anyone else to visit her? No, I think it's just me.

She hadn't noticed how much her mother had shrunk in the last few years. Her mother was never a big woman, but now she's lying in the middle of the bed like a worn-out, faded rag doll. A doll attached to wires and tubes on all sides, a pathetic female imitation of Leonardo da Vinci's Vitruvian Man. Laura, says her mother's new voice. She moves closer. She really shouldn't put off getting glasses any longer. She has to get really close to see her mother's open eyes. Close enough to smell her rancid skin. They've disinfected her mother, but she's still half rotten. The humanity of her mother's body resisting chemical products and technology with dignity. Exhaling the truth that the living smell bad, worse still at the end. Laura, her mother's voice again. Calm down, Mom. You mustn't strain. She likes this. Now she has power. She can use a prescription to mask her inability to hear what her mother has to say. Calm down, don't say what I don't want to hear, it's for your own good. But her mother won't give up that easily. Laura, the voice again. And then, Sorry. She doesn't reply. But her eyes say. Never. I'm never going to forgive you. What she actually says is, Visiting hours are over. I have to go.

And she leaves, almost tiptoeing out. The nurse stops her. The doctor wants to talk to you, she says. Sorry, but I have to go to work. I'll be back tomorrow. My mother won't be out of here that soon, right? She lets out a little laugh at her own joke. The doctor can wait until tomorrow. She knows she's cementing an awful image of herself. But it's good for them to have someone to hate. That way they don't have to hate the patients who remind them how impotent the gilded medical certificates hanging on the wall are.

When she stands in front of the blue-tailed boss she's a normal daughter again. The boss feigns concern. How's your mother? She's still in the ICU, but she's going to be all right. I've just come from there. Yes, she's a perfect daughter. Now he fakes an intimacy they've never shared. And how about you? I'm fine. Wouldn't you like to take a few days off? No, I might if I could stay with my mother in the hospital, but they only allow five-minute visits. I'd rather work and keep my head busy. Plus, I need to finish that article for the next issue of the magazine. Right. Now she isn't just the perfect daughter, she's the perfect employee as well. She's the best.

Her colleagues take turns to traipse past her desk. Pursed lips. They'll spare her today. Even the silver-haired wolf stoops in front of her, every hair out of line. How are you? And squeezes the tips of her fingers. She knows he'll give her ass a tap as soon as she stands up. Sometimes she almost gives in to the tedium and the temptation to take him to the hell of her sexuality. After a night with her, would he still have that look that says, I'm going to make art out of your sketch?

Of course he would. And she'd become a Reichian discourse in the ear of the next Little Red Riding Hood. Looking at the hand he's squeezing, oh, what solidarity. He sees her broken nail. No, not one, all of them. How did she miss that? How could she fail to notice something that wasn't a mere detail? Her fingernails denounce her. He'll obviously say something. What happened? I had to help carry my mother, you know, after she had the heart attack. It's incredible how much people weigh when they're unconscious. So much has happened that I haven't even had time to file my nails. I was sitting in the ICU all night. He understands. So much that he wants to take her out to lunch. She's thin. Pretty, but too thin. She needs to eat. She flashes her best delighted smile, by way of thanks. She's magnanimous today. I can't. You know, I've got this huge article to finish. I need to get on with work while my mother's still in the hospital, because when she's discharged I'm going to have to care for her at home. He walks away, saying that she knows where to find him if she changes her mind.

Now that everyone has played their roles with the utmost competence, she can get down to work. As usual, she forgets where she is while she's writing. Writing is a place she can inhabit. It's comforting to write about other people's lives. It's the best thing about being a journalist. Writing about a reality that doesn't have to become fiction to be articulated.

Then the letters become worms squirming out of my broken nails. What's happening? White and fat, they crawl toward the keys. Some run on their rolling suckers. They get in through the holes and contaminate the computer. Now I infect the screen. I want to call the magazine's tech support to tell them my computer has a virus. But my mouth is full of larvae. And my hands are gone.

07

She used to like having me in her bed. The double bed, where my father should have been, but where I slept instead. When my father came home from work, the sun coming in through the slits in the blind, he used to find my flesh curled up, blocking the way to my mother's body. She had nightmares, she would say. I had to bring her into our bed. I don't know exactly when he gave up. At first, he would just go and sleep on the blue sofa in the sitting room, then one day he switched to the narrow bed in my room, and that was that.

Time was muddled when I was a girl. As the days went by, I ended up believing that it had always been that way. There was no anger in my father's eyes. Only fatigue. And a dispiritedness that was hard to see because it hurt. He looked at me with love and seemed to want to touch me, but my mother was always watching. Always ready to snatch my father's caring gesture out of the air with her teeth. It was easier because he worked nights as a watchman at a pharmaceutical factory. My father was the ghost that didn't frighten us.

He would wake up with the hard sun coming in through all the windows. It's funny how much my mother liked the sun, she who could be mistaken for a fungus, small and humid but with omnipresent tentacles. The house was always really sunny, as if light could mask the crimes committed there. My father would get up, put on his brown stay-at-home pants, open the refrigerator, and take out the plate of food she always left for him. My mother would be around, somewhere, but she wouldn't come. I would sit at the other end of the Formica kitchen table and watch him eat. He used to chew each mouthful loads and loads of times, and one day he explained that you had to chew each mouthful ninety-eight times to help your stomach digest your food and stay healthy. I was relieved. So that was why he didn't talk to me. I didn't really want him to talk, anyway. I don't know if that was when it started, but I was always afraid of words. Of words said out loud. I preferred to sit there, sharing my father's silence.

It never lasted long. My mother would appear at the kitchen door with an accusatory look in her eye and send me away to do something. He never complained. I think my father gave up on me before I was even born. He only used his teeth to chew each bite of food ninety-eight times. Maybe that's why it took so many chews. My father needed to shred some flesh with his teeth. Was he thinking about my mother when he sunk his canines into the chicken breast? The tripe? The beef neck?

Into me?

I really pitied him. And since then, I've felt that way toward all men. I felt as if I could touch my father's fragility with the tips of my fingers, but I never had the courage to bridge the gap that had always existed between us. In some way, I knew that my father was my mother's fatal victim. And because I was an extension of her flesh, he was my victim too.

I wanted to tell him to run away, but I couldn't bear the thought of living without his vague presence. When I managed to slip away from my mother, I fled to my Flicts. That's what I privately called him, ever since I'd read a book about a color which didn't have a place, a color that didn't exist in boxes of colored pencils. I used to watch him doing things with his hands. And I would sit in a corner watching my father do manual tasks. He made a world out of wood, cardboard, and pieces of aluminum. It was a playful world, but I wasn't allowed to play. My mother used to say that my father didn't like me getting involved in his world. And he never contradicted her. He never said anything.

But one day, when he'd finished fixing the bridge over the castle's moat, he changed. It was actually pretty nice, that medieval castle. He called out to me in a voice two octaves higher than usual. Laura. Come here. I emerged from my den like a little mouse and walked hesitantly over to his desk. Come and see. When I got close, he lifted me onto his lap. Look, this is your castle. I made it for you so you won't ever forget that you're a princess. But you must only open the drawbridge if you're sure the person outside means well. My mind went blank. Later on I realized that what I'd felt was happiness.

I would have liked the story to end there. I wanted to tell my father that we should run inside the castle and leave my mother outside. Are there alligators in the moat? I asked. There are massive alligators with pointy teeth. If anyone tried to get across the moat, would the alligators eat them? They'd tear them to shreds. The alligators eat bad people. They eat mothers too, I thought.

08

She's scratching at the door with her curved nails. I tried to cut her nails in the hospital, but it was impossible. The scissors broke, and the nails are still there. Yellowed. Everlasting. I know what she wants. My mother knows I'm writing because she always senses everything. She knows I've found a way to get her out of me without bleeding. She's kind of scared of me now. And I like how this scrap of power feels. I'm the one telling the story, I want to yell. Silence, as usual. Silence, like my father.

It doesn't matter. Now I shout with written words. And there's nothing she can do.

My mother tries. She's anemic. Her kidney doesn't work properly. She can only take a few steps, now that she's got just half a foot. And she's dependent on me for food. But she doesn't give up.

The sound of her nail scratching the door sets my soul on edge, the soul I don't believe I have. Like the teacher's nail wounding the classroom blackboard. Worse.

My mother knows. I woke up with her voice in my head. It's not like that, she was saying. You're telling it all wrong. I want to give my version. I've got a right for my voice to be heard in this story. My heart rate shot up, time stopped for a

moment, and I was paralyzed with fear while her voice tried
to push mine into the shadows. I promised to let her speak.
My heartbeat returned to normal.

But I lied. I'm the one who's talking. This time, it's my
voice. The words are all mine. Mine. I'm the narrator now.
And, for her, the story is over.

09

I don't know how long she stood there. At my father's office door. Her eyes like the lights in a police interrogation. Come to the castle moat, I wanted to say. But deep down I knew that my mother would eat all the alligators, just as she was slowly eating us alive, day by day. I grabbed my father's hand. Let's run inside the castle, I said. I really said it. Just us two, now. But my father wasn't the errant knight with a lion's heart anymore. He was afraid of the black dragon. He just said, Go to your mother. I knew then that we were lost. Leave your father to work in peace, she said. And to him, It's time you got ready for work.

But happiness had snuck in through my pores. And that night I didn't go to her bed. I stayed there in the single bed that was now my father's. When my mother came to get me, I screamed so hard that she was afraid the neighbors would hear. I went back to sleep, victorious. I woke up in the middle of the night. There was no sun coming in through the slits in the blind. I was trapped in the darkness. I couldn't breathe. Had she put me in a box? I shouted. Nothing. I shouted for I don't know how long. Then she came for me. And she carried me to her bed. I could see her satisfaction through the curtain of dry eyes. She had won. Again.

Every time.

She was furious that time. She wanted more. My complete surrender, my blood running through her veins. When I lay in the bed, she opened her nightdress, not caring about the buttons and the indecent noise they made as they pinged onto the floor. I still remember that sound, like drops of water falling on the heads of prisoners until they beg to die. Plink. Plink. Plink. And for me, silence.

It only took me a second to understand what she wanted when she showed me a breast that was large and firm like the rest of her. A white breast that I thought was pretty and terrifying like the rest of her. It smelled of homemade soap like the rest of her. I like to think she forced me, but I know that part of me, the part I disown, wanted that breast.

When my father came home from work, I was still sucking the milk, or whatever it was that would poison me for life. Angrily, hungrily. Unable to escape from her, or from me, he looked at me from the door, and I could feel his horror and his pity. That night in the house on the corner was one of ambiguous feelings. He and I recognized our mutual defeat in the wordless look that crossed the room while she snored, her head on two down pillows. Unlike me, my mother has never had trouble sleeping.

The following morning, the man who was never there wasn't there. He'd abandoned me in the black dragon's stomach where I would go on being digested night after night.

10

The doctor is there when she arrives at the ICU reception desk. She looks like one of those long-legged birds. Her nose is a pointy beak. She's too stiff and upright, she's seen too many dead bodies. The doctor wears white like all the others, but she can still make out the black feathers on her body. So here you are, the doctor says, her ironic smile wrinkling the corners of her mouth. Yes, she says, here I am. She doesn't fear the power of the white coat.

I need to talk to you about your mother. Yes, here I am. She enjoys putting on her best act. Like her mother, she's always been able to sniff out fragility. She knows the doctor is disconcerted by her coldness, her blameless eyes, the apologies she doesn't plan on making. The doctor can't stand death. There she is, bearing witness to death and reaffirming her impotence day after day, but everything she does is an appearance she works hard to maintain. Thin ice that her foot would be all too happy to break. I'm all ears, she says, inwardly celebrating.

The doctor clears her throat with a strangled little cough. She tilts her chin and looks like she's about to take flight. I imagine you're aware of the awful conditions of neglect in which your mother was found. And that the social worker was considering whether to inform the police about your negligence. Sure.

That was the doctor trying to hit her. My mother is independent and perfectly lucid, she lives in a safe building with a security guard, and a doorman there twenty-four hours a day who can be contacted using the intercom. She has a cell phone to call for help. If she didn't call, it's because she didn't want to.

She sees the doctor puff up, more self-assured because she thinks has an explanation. Elderly people don't always manage to call for help. Your mother must not have noticed her health deteriorating. Depression left her unresponsive. Well, well, her mother, depressed. The doctor thinks her mother is the type to be struck by depression. Not even an armored car would knock her down. She makes a point of calling the doctor by the name on her badge. Adriana, I know you're doing the job you're poorly paid by the state to do, but, with all due respect, you don't know my mother. She sees the flutter of alarm in the doctor's featherless chest. She's just kidnapped her title, and now the doctor feels more naked. Let's be objective. I have to get to work, and you must have other patients to see. What was it you wanted to say to me?

The doctor clears her throat again. The nurse sitting at reception is eavesdropping on their conversation. She'll have something to talk about during her coffee break. Fine, if that's the way you want it. That is the way I want it, she says. Just to spite her. The doctor lets her shoulders drop. She's certain that later, alone in the bathroom, the doctor is going to cry. Not yet, though. Your mother has an iron constitution. Any other seventy-year-old in similar circumstances would have died. Now her voice is neutral and professional. But your mother won't survive another episode. She mustn't be left alone anymore. If you can't care for her, you should find someone who can be on hand twenty-four hours a day. Her kidneys are functioning, but badly, and she's anemic. Your mother is going to need prolonged treatment, and she'll have to start a rigid medication regimen. The nutritionist is going to plan a diet, which must be strictly followed. And we're going to put your mother on our list for home visits. She's not the sort of patient who usually needs this kind of care, because she doesn't have a chronic condition, but we want to make sure she's all right.

Plural. The doctor has just made herself plural, but she lets it slide. They're trying to intimidate her. To make sure she won't kill her mother. As if she could. Your mother is a very sweet woman, it's a shame she doesn't have other children, the doctor goes on, more earnestly than she would have thought possible. The psychologist would like to have a word with you. After that, it would be great if you could go through to the social worker's room. If your mother remains stable, she'll be moved out of the ICU today. We plan to keep her under observation for another two days, in a private room. And then, if everything's on track, she'll be free to go.

This time, the doctor hits her target. Two days. She assumed her mother would stay in the hospital for at least two weeks. The black bird turns and walks off down the corridor. She'd like to know how many firm steps those long legs take before giving way, out of range of the nurse who's willing her to fail as she fills in charts.

She hasn't yet recovered from the news about her mother being discharged so soon, when an understanding smile hits her. I'm Dr. Márcia, the psychologist. Since when is a psychologist a doctor? she wonders. She doesn't return the greeting. Would you mind coming to my office for a minute? She follows her. She knows she won't escape today. She'll have to go through the motions with all the white-coated professionals, all so proud of their sterility. How are you? Perhaps you'd like to talk a bit about your feelings. I know it's not easy to deal with your parents going downhill. I can imagine that you might be feeling guilty . . .

How scared she is of those well-intentioned eyes, that mask that says "I care about you because I'm so superior, and I get the horrible creature that you are. And because later on I'll be able to present your case at a conference and write it up for a scientific journal. So, feel free to bear everything and shock my faultless bourgeois morals, you poor dear."

It might be fun to accept that disinterested offer of perfectly professional kindness. She quickly changes tack. She sinks into the chair. Doctor, I'm so glad you're here. There are actually some things I need to get off my chest. I know everyone thinks I'm a neglectful daughter. Maybe I'm even a bad woman. The psychologist's blue eyes grow wide, and she makes to pro-test. No, no, don't say anything. I see the way they look at me. Even, what's that thin doctor's name? The ICU doctor who was talking to me just now. She's constantly accusing me. I understand. How could any of you know? My mother isn't easy to deal with, but I love her all the same. But what you have to understand is that my mother hates me. Ever since I was little, she's blamed me for my father leaving us. My father wasn't a bad man, but he couldn't bear living in those conditions. She sighs. What I'm going to tell you now is difficult to admit. But the truth is, my father couldn't take how filthy our house was.

The filth at least is real. But she needs to reduce it to a filth the psychologist can handle.

She goes on.

My mother never cared about the house or food or me or my father. She just used to stay in bed all day watching TV. When my father came home from work, she would defrost something for him and put it on the table. I sometimes went a week without a bath because my mother thought water removed the skin's natural protection. When my father left, my mother blamed me. She said my father left because he couldn't stand me. From that day on, my mother only got out of bed to play cards with her friends. Every now and again, she would bring a drunk man home, which I found really difficult. One of them tried to grab me once, and it was horrible. I only escaped by running out into the street. My mother never had to work because my grandfather was in the army and left her a lifetime allowance, so she's always done whatever she wanted. She's always been the same. When I got a bit older, I started cleaning the house, and at least then I didn't have to put up with the mess. But my mother carried on being just as spiteful. I couldn't take any more of it, and when I was old enough to leave home, I moved into a boardinghouse for young women downtown. My mother was furious and told me not to visit her. Then about twenty years ago, she banned me from seeing her. I go to her place, all the same. But my mother sends me away. She says I ruined her life. I thought about talking to someone, but who? My mother has always been like this, she's always lived like this. When I call, she hangs up on me. And now this happens.

She's disappointed because the story she's made up is terrible. It makes her seem more pathetic than she could have imagined. No one would believe it, not even that psychologist.

But the psychologist opens her understanding eyes as wide as the gates of heaven. She can read her thoughts. Dr. Márcia feels superior now. Thanks to her competent approach, she's finally managed to make headway in this difficult case. The information is surprising, and the psychologist can't wait to be rid of her so as to run after the doctor and flaunt this new knowledge. Dr. Márcia doesn't tire of telling the medical doctors, who regard her with arrogant condescension, that it's just as important to look after patients' heads as their bodies. But they dismiss her with superior smiles. And now Dr. Márcia has a chance. It's a real turning point in the case. Thanks to the psychologist, thanks above all to her way with people.

I didn't say anything before because, you know, it's hard to denounce your own mother. She uses her index finger to wipe away a real tear that has appeared in the corner of her right eye.

What's that tear for? The psychologist likes the tear. So she likes it too. She maintains her worried expression and a vague air of stupidity. Please, I'm begging you, you have to keep this to yourself. I'd hate for it to become hospital gossip. My mother would never forgive me, you know. And I still live in hope that one day we'll be able to set things straight. I think daughters are like that, aren't we? Now she's evoking complicity with the younger woman. The psychologist must surely have problems with her own mother as well. We can forgive the person who brought us into the world for anything, don't you think?

She likes what she sees in the psychologist's face. Most of all she likes branding her aseptic mother as a pig. Her mother, no less, who was pretty much born holding an alcohol wipe and made her wash her hands every half hour. Even today, her hands are reddened by the rough homemade soap and its smell will always be stuck in her nose. She could bathe in Chanel No. 5 and still not smell like Marilyn Monroe. The smell of her mother's soap, made to disinfect all the world's filth, emanates from her.

An idea begins to take shape now. Why didn't she think of this before? Facing the Bambi-eyed psychologist, she knows just what she has to do.

11

She's getting ready to take the leap. She can't mess up now. She's sure the moment's right. You can't imagine how glad I am to finally have someone to talk to. I've got plenty of friends. That's a lie, she hasn't got any. But it's hard to admit that my own mother would rather die alone than let me help her. At work, everyone wants to know what happened to my mother, but when something like this happens in your family, you have to be discreet. I was brought up to guard my family's secrets. That's the truth. I'm ashamed, you know. My mother told me so often that everything was my fault and that I messed up when I came into her life, I think I ended up believing it.

The psychologist is entranced. She moves forward. She wants to cross her fingers but retreats under the table. I don't know how to solve this. What do you think? Yes, she has to make it seem like it's the doctor's idea. When my mother goes back home, she's not going to want me near her. She's never wanted a maid, not even a cleaning lady. I read once that compulsively collecting trash is a kind of pathology. Is that right? The psychologist is trusting her more and more. My mother will swear to you that she'll do everything by the book, but it'll be a lie. And I won't be able to do anything to stop her because she's an independent woman. And then it'll happen again, and maybe next time my mother won't survive. I feel powerless. Trapped.

This time, she starts sobbing. She didn't plan this. Where are the tears coming from? She knows the tears are real. She's not that good an actress. Why is she crying? Because she resembles her mother more than she'd like? No, her mother would never do what she's doing. Her mother is a shocking human being, but she's never deceived anyone about who she is. She's paid the price for all her weirdness without complaint. She at least needs to say that in her mother's favor. Now she's crying so much that tears splash onto the floor. She's horrified when she realizes that there's snot dripping from her nose. The psychologist hands her the box of tissues, which she thoughtfully keeps on her desk. She must buy the tissues herself. It's one of the sacrifices she makes for her patients while she waits for a promotion to the private wing, where she could have peach-toned office décor and hug relatives without fear of dirtying her clothes. She blows her nose noisily. The psychologist offers some platitude about it being good to get all her feelings out. She nods and sniffs.

What do you think I should do? she asks, skillfully picking up the thread again.

The psychologist's face shows a competent mix of compunction and professionalism, and her voice now sounds like Für Elise piped out of a gas truck's loudspeaker. Look, it's a difficult decision to make. But perhaps we should start thinking about . . . She likes the plural, the appearance of that plural is a good omen for her plans. Perhaps the best thing for your mother right now would be some kind of limited interdiction. You know, something that lets you take the necessary steps and look after her best interests. It's a very tough decision, I know, but it would protect your mother from herself. It would absolutely be for her own good.

The psychologist fell for it. She needs to be very careful now not to scare the fox who's just put her paw in the snare. She's almost there. A moment longer and the fox will be dangling from the top of the tree. She lifts her salty eyes and shakes her head. She has to get the tone just right. No more, no less. Le mot juste, as Flaubert would say. Questions are always better. Do you mean, what's it called . . . a legal interdiction?

The psychologist opens her mouth to speak, but she can't chance it. I have a friend who had to do that when her father got Alzheimer's and started to run away from home, but making that decision was really hard on her. Everything's fine now, but it was really tough at the start. I'm not sure I'd be strong enough to go through with that. A bit of selfishness will make her more convincing. The psychologist maintains her most professional expression. She's getting more relaxed, she even leans back in the chair. It's certainly not an easy decision. But we think it would be in your mother's best interest. This is sometimes the way it goes with elderly people.

Now she shakes her head a bit less vehemently. Well, if you think it's the right thing to do, maybe I'll have to start facing up to it. Even though my mother hasn't been the mother I dreamed of, it's not fair for her life to end like that. If it's for her own good, I know I have to be strong. After all, I'm all my mother has. And she lifts her shoulders bravely. Then lets them fall. But I don't even know how you do something like that. The psychologist's tone of voice is increasingly protective. Let me ask the social worker, informally of course, how families normally go about it. In her line of work, she must have seen a few cases like this over the years. I assume you'll have to present medical reports documenting your mother's temporary incapacity to look after herself. In my opinion, the facts speak for themselves, so it won't be difficult to prove that this is a necessary step. You can take time to get used to the idea while I make arrangements with our team. Strictly speaking, we shouldn't get involved with this, but your mother is here with us, and we're going to help her. You'll need a lawyer, of course. Maybe you know someone already? No, she doesn't. But she'll find one. She pushes her luck further. I don't even know how to break this kind of news to my mother. Sweetheart, says the psychologist, putting her hand on her arm, I'll be with you all the way. Believe me, you're not alone. The fox is now dangling by her paw from the top of the tree. And as she looks up at her, she wipes a real tear from her eye with her sleeve.

She leaves the room feeling light. As light as anyone in her position can be. She's almost happy. Happy enough that she can see her mother. She even wants to see her mother. The nurse at reception looks at her with fearful respect. She flashes a sorrowful half smile, trapped now inside her new character.

Her mother's weaselly eyes are open. Her mother knows what she's done. She always does. You're being discharged from the ICU today. You can go home in two days. I'm getting the apartment cleaned. Do you forgive me? asks her mother, her voice torn by the tube they stuck down her throat on the first day. She flashes a smile that's almost wicked. I'm going to look after you now. It'll be better that way. I hope you'll coop-erate when they give you the news. How dare she talk to her mother like that?

She feels power spreading out from her body like long fin-gers with long nails that her mother can surely see. And then she notices her mother's hand on the white sheet. The hand looks so small. She hesitates, but she can't refute the appear-ance of that hand. She knows that her mother has claws. Her mother's hand crawls toward hers like one of those spiders in the garden. She realizes that she and her mother have nails that are shaped the same. She and her mother don't look alike. She's sure she looks like her father. But there's no escaping the shape of their nails.

She gets up, brusquely, and leaves the ICU without saying goodbye. She almost runs. I think my mother is improving, she says to the nurse at reception in her best attentive-daughter voice. Then she can't do it anymore. When she's out of the woman's line of sight, she starts running. She bounds down the ten flights of stairs. She knows she'll never be able to run enough.

She looks for a bathroom on the ground floor. She opens the door wide and slams it on the fingers of her left hand. The pain is hideous, but she's beyond pain. A short woman carrying a packet of geriatric diapers under her arm asks if she needs help, if she wants her to call a nurse. She can't speak. She shakes her head to say no. She looks at her nails, which are starting to blacken. They're still her mother's nails.

12

Ever since my father left me, my heart had been beating down in my stomach. It beat with hate. Then it resounded with regret. My father had been ground down first, but I was mostly to blame. I was the one who should have looked after him. And I'd failed. And then that. How could I? I washed and washed and washed with so much soap in the first few days until I understood that I would never get clean, that cleanliness would always be out of reach. And the soap smelled of her, and the more I washed, the more my body became hers. Because the soap was her filth. The cleaner, the dirtier.

There was nothing left for me. I rattled around inside the house and felt tied to her body like a dog on a choke chain. In my case it wasn't a chain, it was an umbilical cord. I gradually became unable to distinguish my body from hers. And when I ate, I didn't know whose mouth the food went into or whose ass it came out of. I started to do worse at school, because when I picked up my pencil, we used to write in pencil back then, I was shocked to see her hand. I erased everything, all the time. The only thing I liked doing was erasing. And one day I erased my whole year's work, page after page. And when the teacher tried to stop me, I bit her hand.

They took me to the headmistress and called my mother. She's like this because her father left, my mother said. It'll pass. She's a very sensitive girl. The headmistress said I'd be expelled if I carried on being so aggressive. She only let me stay because I'd previously been so calm. I just needed to erase things. Before we left, my mother bent down in front of me, grabbed my face with her two hands that were identical to mine, and said, If you do anything stupid like that again, I swear, I won't let you come to school anymore. I'll teach you at home.

I didn't know that it was illegal. So I believed her. It wouldn't have made a difference if I'd known, because my mother was the law. Not even God could compete with her, I knew that. School was the furthest my fleshy chain let me go Monday through Friday. I stopped erasing. And I didn't look at my hands when I wrote, just at the board. Much later, this helped me become an excellent typist. People are always surprised how fast I can type without looking at the keyboard. And without any typos. But I still did badly on my exams, because then I had to look at the paper and I saw my hands. I flunked that year. And I would have flunked the next if my teacher hadn't noticed that I knew the answers but just couldn't write them. She started doing oral exams with me. She was a thin young woman with long, lank hair who wore brightly colored clothes and necklaces, fresh out of college and keen to save the world. Mediocrity stifled her, but it hadn't broken her yet. And she was curious.

That same teacher noticed that the hair on my arms had fallen out. I hadn't realized myself because I used to avoid looking at my body, which was my mother's. She called my mother, who didn't give it much thought. Who needs hair? she said to the shocked teacher.

Then my eyelashes started to fall out, followed by my eyebrows. The other girls chased me at recess and threw chinaberry fruit at me, which sometimes got stuck in my ears. I didn't mind because I liked the feeling of foreign objects. But after a while they stopped, because my apathy ruined the game. I was so humorless that even making jokes at my expense was no fun. They left me in my corner, where I could feel my mother's gastric juices digesting me.

When I started to go bald, my mother began to worry. She made me wear a hat that she'd knitted. But the boy who sat behind me in class pulled it off on the second day, and everyone could see that I was bald. At the teacher's insistence, the headmistress called my mother, who promised to take me to the doctor. The teacher started asking me questions. I think my father left because he didn't like me. I think it's better not having hair on my body. Yes, I'm sure my mother doesn't hit me. No, I don't have an uncle or a grandfather who sits me on his lap. I only have my mother.

I don't have a body, I tried to say. But the words wouldn't come out. She'd trapped all the words inside me before I was born. And before that, she'd trapped my father's words. She didn't have words herself. We were a wordless family. With a single body. The doctor touched me, and I didn't like it. I preferred it when the other kids threw chinaberry fruit at me. They did dozens of tests, they took loads of blood samples, and I did like that bit. I liked the prick of the needle. Nothing unusual has shown up, the doctor said. The tests are all normal. She's healthy. It might just be an emotional reaction. Has she gone through any trauma recently?

Only her father leaving, my mother said. The doctor was relieved. He had a diagnosis.

That was the first time I took antidepressants. And tranquilizers. But back then, I didn't know the names. I got really sleepy, which was the effect they were going for. I slept like a drunk in class. And my whole body remained hairless. The teacher had talked to my classmates while I was away having the tests, so they didn't pull my hat off anymore. Less as a result of the teacher explaining that I had an emotional disorder brought on by my father leaving and more because I grossed them out. No one wanted to touch me. They said I smelled funny. Now that I think about it, I suppose they somehow smelled the milk.

I felt the teacher's gaze on me. I don't mind not having hair, I said to her one day. Because I liked her, and I didn't want her to worry. It wasn't worth her worrying. And I was afraid that if my mother didn't trust the teacher, she might swallow her as well. But early one morning, she stopped me in the corridor and said that the two of us wouldn't be going to class that day. The tone of her voice scared me, and I said I wanted to go to class. She said she needed to take me to a really nice place and that I could trust her. I liked her and didn't want her to feel hurt, but nor did I want to go anywhere, not even a nice place. Even so, she tugged me by the arm and led me out into the street, to her car. The teacher's car smelled of chewing gum. Tutti-frutti.

She took me to a different clinic, where there were loads of toys on the floor. And a doctor who seemed to be friends with the teacher started talking to me. She said I could choose whatever toy I wanted, and I chose a big doll to play with. When I pulled his dummy out, he cried and said, Mommy. Then the doctor with the kind face started asking me weird questions. To start with, I didn't say anything, but the teacher said I needed to answer her questions. I stared, saying yes or no. Just yes or no. I figured that yes or no was all right, yes or no wouldn't do any harm. Do you play with other children? No. Do you drink milk? Yes. Do you eat meat and vegetables? Yes. Do you have other relatives? No. Do you miss your dad? No. I don't know why, but I wanted to lie. Why did your dad leave? No. No what? No. You don't know? I didn't answer. Did your dad used to cuddle you? No. Did he used to touch you? No. Do you sleep in your bed? No. Where do you sleep? I didn't answer. Do you sleep with your mom? Yes. Are you scared of sleeping on your own? Yes. Does your mom touch you when you sleep together? No. Do you touch your mom? I didn't answer. I didn't know if that was touching. What do you and your mom do when you're in bed and you're not sleeping? I didn't answer.

The teacher took my hand, looked right into my eyes, and I felt a warm feeling that I wished wouldn't stop. You can answer, I swear nothing bad is going to happen to you if you answer. I didn't answer. Then she said. Honey, this lady is a doctor. She's used to listening to everything children say to her, even things that seem really bad. You can say anything you like. It was because of the "honey" that I said what was so hard to say. And I don't even know what made it so hard to say, because I thought it was normal, I'd seen lots of babies doing that with their mothers. I just felt like that, made dirty by soap. Come on, honey, you need to tell us.

At night I suck my mom's booby. And then I go to sleep. My dad left because he was the one who should have been sucking it, not me.

And then I felt like I needed to explain. I don't know why. My dad didn't like it when I was in the bed, but there was room for him, and I really wanted him to get in. I tried not to go to my mom's bed because he didn't like it, but my mom came looking for me when it was dark and I was on my own. So I stayed there with her booby. And my dad left.

And do you like her booby? Do you like sucking your mom's booby? The teacher had left the room. I only noticed when the door banged shut. The doctor had a kind face, she looked right into my eyes.

No. Yes.

13

That was the first time I ever felt sorry for my mother. I don't know what they said to her at school, but that night I heard her crying. I didn't know my mother could cry. Where had she hidden her tears for all those years? I thought everyone had a big bag of tears in their belly. Because when I cried, it always started in my belly and worked its way up to my eyes. I thought my mother had been born without a tear bag and that was why she didn't cry.

That night I slept in my father's bed, which before that had been mine and was now mine again. I was really scared and tried to go to my mother's bed in the middle of the night, but she pushed me away, saying that thanks to my big mouth I could never sleep there again. And I knew I shouldn't have believed the teacher or the doctor with the nice face, because words are bad.

I never drank milk again, and even now, as an adult, I don't drink it. I lie and say I'm lactose intolerant, and people leave me in peace. I stopped talking to the teacher, I only answered her questions in class with monosyllables. At first she looked hurt. I think she wanted me to idolize her for having saved me. But she didn't save me, we both knew that. To save me, she would've had to go way beyond good intentions, she would've had to plunge both hands into the world's guts. I know now that getting involved with children like me means permanently sacrificing some kind of innocence. The teacher was a good person and preferred to still see a good person reflected in the bathroom mirror. I don't blame her. If I'd had a choice, I would've done the same.

After a while the teacher forgot about me. There's no shortage of children to save. Children with problems that don't make you nauseated. I knew I was the kind of child people would rather forget. If they could, they would've packed me off to another school so they didn't have to look at me every day. And remember what everyone knew in the end. Quiet and strange. With no hair and wearing a hat that made me look like a cotton swab. As clean as it was dirty. No, I didn't look like a honey.

Other teachers came along. I got older and learned that I could live pretty much in peace if I did the things other people thought were important and did nothing to draw attention to myself. The hair started to grow back on my body, but I stayed bald. And with time, people stopped caring about my bald head, which I covered with a hat even in summer. I don't think I suffered so much then. I lived inside myself and went about my days like a sleepwalker, oblivious to the outside world. Whoever faces great loss knows that there's a certain relief in not expecting any good to come, in not hoping for anything. I was a child, but I lived like an adult who had lost a lot. It was better that way. Me and my mother in our quiet routine. It was possible to live without believing that life was a great miracle.

One night, my mother came to my bed and asked if I wanted to sleep with her again. I didn't want to anymore but, in the end, I accepted the hand she held out to me because that was what I always did. It was still dark, but the moon was visible through the slits in the blind, and we looked at each other for a while under the filter of the moonlight. I lowered my eyes to her breasts. And then I looked down at mine, which were getting hard under my nightdress. Did my mother want to suck my breasts?

I wanted her to suck them. And I wanted to suck hers. But we were both scared. And we went to sleep together with our breasts between us. So there was something we wanted, after all. And that caused the tension in our house with the words that couldn't be said. Back then, I hated my mother with a different kind of hate. The body that was never mine was increasingly hers. I felt dirty. I started washing my hands as much as she did. Mother and daughter in that house on the corner, furiously washing their hands. It was always a surprise when the sun came in through the slits in the blind.

A few days later, I woke up in that bed and didn't recognize my body anymore, or hers. I screamed that I'd become a giant cockroach, and I hadn't even read Kafka at that point. I curled up into a fetal position because I knew it wasn't my body or hers. I had no body at all, and I was sure of that when I felt liquid soaking the bed. I was finally dissolving, and I was suddenly relieved. You peed the bed, my mother said. And it was true. It was just pee, not my whole being.

After cleaning myself up, I opened the cupboard where my mother kept her collection of steak knives. There were ones with bone, wood, plastic, and silver handles. My mother liked knives. So did I. I chose the prettiest one, with a bone handle in the shape of a sphinx. And I crept up behind her. I got close. I'm going to kill you, I said wordlessly. She focused her empty eyes. And she ignored me. I spent that whole day following her around the house with the knife. Wherever she went, I was there behind her with the knife. And I stayed there with the knife while she washed and swept and cleaned and rubbed alcohol over everything.

She came up to me in the middle of the afternoon, her eyes expressionless. She stopped right at the tip of my knife. She bent down so the tip rested where her heart was. Go on. Stab me. I saw that her heart and her breast were the same. I stabbed. Her flesh was softer than I'd imagined. I saw the bloody mouth spit. And I couldn't do it anymore. I let the knife fall to the floor. She laughed, and the sound of her laughter hurt my ears so much that I wished I was deaf. You're like your father. Weak. I couldn't even cry. Now she was hooting with laughter. The indecent sound of the air whistling through her teeth curdled my blood. Not again, I thought. Not again.

Slowly, breathing heavily from the effort of running to the place beyond fear, I picked up the knife from the floor. And with the courage I didn't have when it came to stabbing her, I opened a red smile in my stomach. In one go. I watched the laughter dry up between her yellow teeth.

So there was a way to separate myself from her.

14

Her mother is behaving herself. When they tell her about the interdiction, she just blinks. It's for your own good, says the psychologist-with-the-Für-Elise-voice. Her mother is more afraid of psychologists than she is. She just blinks. Is her mother there? She conquers her repulsion and places her bandaged hand on her mother's head. I'm going to look after you, she says. I'm going to move in with you so I can look after you. She's playing her role well. Her mother just blinks. Is she scared? What happened to your hand? her mother asks.

Her mother is there in that body, it's clear now. Her mother has just announced her presence. And she's trampling on her even before she's left her hospital bed. But she's not going to allow it. This is her best chance. Yes, I'm bound to your body, but right now you're in more pain than I am. And I can cause you unimaginable pain, even if it means dying with you. That's what she thinks. But what she says is, I trapped my hand in the bathroom door, you know, with all this stuff on my mind. But it's fine. The important thing now is to look after you properly.

In the corner of the room, the doctor is the only one who seems to understand that nothing there is fine. She's not convinced. But what can she do? Life stinks, everyone dies in the end, and these two have survived so far without her intervention.

Facing her mother, in the middle of the scene, she knows she can always count on other people's selfishness. It never fails. It's better for everyone to believe. An argument is enough, even if it is full of holes, and they'll cling to it by their nails. Grateful to be able to keep pretending they're not fakers. Her mother too? She wonders, but there's no time left for answers. When she helps her mother into the taxi that's waiting for them outside the hospital, they're alone. Alone as usual. More alone than ever.

Three-and-a-half hours later, she begins the second act.

She knocks on the blue-tailed boss's office door, and now she's as good as him. That metaphor about the fight, he says. She interrupts. I know you don't like my metaphors, but it's the last time you'll have to put up with them. She laughs a friendly laugh. I'm going to have to leave the magazine. He opens his eyes wide. Is it surprise? Or relief? He thinks she's competent but strange, she knows that. There are countless ways that a reasonably attractive woman with access to decent shops, decent cosmetics, and a decent hairdresser can cover up the sordidness of her own body. But there's a diffuse strangeness that remains. And it's only picked up by the moribund animal in each person. That's what makes people keep their distance. She knows that.

My mother is in a lot of pain. We're a small family and we only have each other. I thought about it a lot, it's a difficult decision for me, but my mother needs more help than a hired caregiver can provide. I'm going to have to stop work for a while so I can concentrate on helping her get better. I'm planning on giving up my apartment and moving into hers. The boss makes to speak, but she needs to go on. My mother has a small allowance, which will cover the bills. But I'll really need my wage guarantee fund. It'll give us something to live off until things settle down and I can get back to my normal life. I know it's a difficult time and the magazine is cutting back, but it would be a real help if you could fire me. She stops talking. He opens his mouth to speak but doesn't say anything. She knows she's left him with no choice. And now she's the best of all daughters, the best of all women, an exceptional human being. She's not an odd employee anymore, she's dedicated. She deserves to have the company do its best for her. And so she leaves, redeemed. No one can even gossip about someone so altruistic. It's a good parting image, in case she ever needs to go back.

Four hours and fifteen minutes later, she begins the last act. The second to last, in fact, but she has no way of knowing that yet.

The cleaners did a great job, don't you think? she says to her mother when they enter the room. It doesn't even look as if you were rotting in here. Her mother blinks. Then asks to have a bath. She's never given her mother a bath before. She'd feared this moment, but now she feels nothing. Not even disgust. She doesn't recognize those breasts. That raisin-like body is another. She's not there. Nor is her mother. A young woman bathes an old woman. They're not them.

She helps her mother into the nightdress that smells of her soap. And now she recognizes her. She fumblingly gets her mother into bed. She answers her mother's mute question. No. I'm going to sleep in the guest room. And she laughs, it's funny to think of her mother having guests. The room was supposed to be for her, but she was already grown up when her mother sold the house on the corner and bought the apartment. She's never slept there. Until today. She feels something squeezing her wrist. On her good side, not her bandaged hand. She looks at her mother's wizened hand, the nails yellow and indestructible. I don't like you touching me, she says. Her mother doesn't let go. What are you doing? her mother asks with her damaged voice. I'm looking after you. Repaying your dedication to me. Don't be ungrateful, Mommie dear.

She gives her mother a sleeping tablet. But every time she goes down the corridor, she feels her mother's eyes on her. How many tablets will she have to shove into her mother's mouth to shake the feeling of those eyes following her around the apartment? She gathers up her things in her room. It's a room with old, solid furniture. Good furniture. A door connects her room to her mother's. She shuts the door. And when she opens it again, her mother is standing in front of her. She feels like a child again. Impotent in the face of her mother's power. She's less than a meter tall now. Her mother senses her doubt. She composes herself. Go back to bed, Mom. You can't keep wandering about. But, oh yes, her mother can. She's only got one-and-a-half feet, and she can.

She realizes that, in fact, she's the fox dangling from the top of the tree. It's her. With her help, her mother tricked everyone. And she gave her mother a bath. And she lives in her mother's apartment. And she's living off her mother's allowance. And she has no life but her mother's. Get away from me. Don't you dare come near me. She slams the door in her mother's face. She pushes the armchair up against the door. As soon as it gets light, she's going to call the locksmith and ask him to install new locks between her and her mother.

I'm going to die, she thinks. I can't breathe. I'm suffocating. She drags herself to her bag and takes out her computer. There is something she can do. Something she has to do. She starts writing. Laura, says her mother with her nails. Blood runs into the keyboard. Chapter One is born bloodstained.

15

I'd been told that writers were a sort of god. They created a world in which they could live, escaping out of this one through the back door. I spent my whole life preparing to be a god. It's just that what I'm doing now is uninventing myself. I think that's it. Reality is a fiction. And when I write, I'm destroying the creature that's been sculpted with love and desperation. It's the opposite. I have to destroy my human form to get at the stone.

I can feel her there on the other side of the door. And she's not even scratching anymore. That mother with one-and-a-half feet. I cook for her. I put food into her mouth so I don't have to see her hands. She sits on a little stool in the bath, and I wash her with a cloth. I don't look, I just do it. I feel as if she's disconnecting from her ailing body, and she hasn't even insisted on washing her hands with her soap. It's like the illness has kidnapped her body and she's simply dragging it along, a carcass she's resigned herself to living with but which is no longer part of her. She's distancing herself from her body, and it seems she's in all the eyes that watch me. She's stopped asking if I forgive her. Sometimes she says my name to herself. Laura. I pretend not to hear.

This passivity is new, and it scares me. What's she cooking up? What evil does she have in store for me? I bought a flat-screen TV and installed it in front of her bed. My mother never liked TV, but I'm not giving her a choice. I just switch it on so I don't have to hear her nails, which no longer scratch my door, or her voice, which no longer speaks. I switch on the TV and leave her there while I write, locked in my new room. Alzira-from-the-spiritualist-center came to visit her and thought everything was fine. My mother asked about the spirits and the center's charity work, and Alzira went away happy with what she thought had been a great conversation. She was so happy to talk about herself that she failed to notice that my mother didn't open her mouth. Alzira's not a bad person. Just naive. She still looks at me mistrustfully, out of the corner of her eye, but she's starting to think that maybe I'm a good daughter. After all, who else would leave their "glamorous journalist's life" to shut herself in an old apartment with her sick mother? Aren't I great.

These bedroom walls are suffocating me. I tell my mother I'm going out. If you need me, just call me on the cell phone. I've left it on your bedside table. She says have a nice walk, as if we were a normal family. Do normal families exist?

I'm glad you went out. I take only shallow breaths, but I could feel your presence in the air, and it was suffocating me. Don't kid yourself, I too feel your eyes and your still-young nails scratching at my door. You, my girl, give me supernatural powers simply because you're scared of your own strength. You've always been afraid to take responsibility for your own desire, ever since you were small. Cowardice and evil were yours too. I'm writing for your readers. But it's your decision whether to publish my version alongside yours. It'll always be your decision. I won't let you chalk up another act of violence to me.

This time you're going to have to assume responsibility. You have to choose whether you'll kill me or not in your narrative. If you kill me, you'll know that my voice is there, somewhere, even if you burn the notebook and no one knows where exactly. Yes, because I can only write by hand. And I think there's more courage in writing by hand, weighing up every letter. It requires effort, and words don't appear and disappear on a screen as if they could simply come into being or be wiped out at no cost. Your father scarcely knew how to write, don't kid yourself. You inherited your talent from me.

I don't want you all to think I'm good, because I'm not. I'm just old. And very, very tired. It's strange that my daughter thinks I spent weeks dragging myself to the refrigerator until there was nothing left to eat because I wanted to hurt her. Her. Or that I didn't pay the electricity bill because I wanted to be in the dark. Or that I liked watching the cat devouring my foot. Or that I enjoyed pissing and shitting myself. Me of all people, when I've always been so clean. I've never said the words piss or shit before. They're not my words. No, they are. I have to be careful not to make myself better than I am. Or worse. But I was always prudish when it came to words. Fart, for example, is a difficult word for me. Fart fart fart. That's it, I'm liberating myself as well.

I don't even know why I didn't call for help. I know my daughter thinks it was to punish her, and the few others who know me think it was out of pride. I've always been a proud woman, that's true, but when it happened, I just felt so tired. Too tired even to react. I was exhausted from the effort of all those years, decades. I felt time's teeth on my body and I gave up. I just gave up. I stopped trying.

That was all it was. I didn't mean to hurt anyone, and I didn't want to die. I just couldn't be bothered anymore. But the body doesn't give up without making some kind of scene, and, well, you know what happened next.

I don't think she needed to kill the cat. I know she did it. I know she must have enjoyed it. She hated the cat because the cat liked me. Did the cat like how my flesh tasted? Maybe you think it odd that I call him the cat instead of using his name. But Cat was his name, I never gave him another one. If I could have, I wouldn't even have given Laura a name. If it were up to me, she would have been Girl. But her father said that was crazy, and we wouldn't be allowed to register her name as Girl. Back then I still listened to him, so I called her Laura, which was the name of a chicken in a children's story that someone called Clarice Lispector wrote not long before she was born. I've never read anything else by that author, but I felt compelled to buy the book when I saw it in the bookstore window when I was pregnant and sensed I was going to have a girl. The Secret Life of Laura. It didn't seem much like a story for children, but it echoed the strangeness of the creature inside me, eating me from the inside for nine months. I don't remember who said it, but that's what a child is: "The one who entered my house but didn't come in from outside." And, if it's a girl, then the whole thing's darker still.

I must be a more normal old woman than I thought, because I've already started rambling. I just wanted to explain why the cat was Cat. I tried to look into the animal's gray eyes when he started eating my foot, but he wouldn't look up at me. He'd always been so gentle, and I don't think he wanted me to see the wild beast in him. The truth is that I didn't mind at the time. The pain made me pass out and let me forget for a while. It's incredible how we manage to block out even what hurts us. And it did hurt. A lot. But what did I think? That the cat would die passively with me, as if he were Romeo and I his Juliet? Hunger was driving him crazy, so he did what nature taught him to do. Didn't I spend my life devouring Laura? Oh, she's going to love that sentence.

The key in the lock. Laura's back. I thought she'd be out longer, that she'd go to the movies. Laura's mad about movies. I never understood how anyone can

16

I'm not sure where to go. I leave the apartment, start walking, and, the next thing I know, I'm in front of the bookstore. The biggest one of all. A modern architectural project, frequented by university students, the books strategically lit like bullets in shiny packaging. I always find it hard to leave the apartment. However threatening the apartment is, if we know what to expect, even pain can be comforting. And I've learnt that the worst path is better than an unknown one. I want to turn back, but it would seem like defeat. I carry on wandering aimlessly among all those people. Even though I'm just another nobody roaming anonymously among the shelves of books, and I feel like I shouldn't be there. So many things have been written, so many people are writing. Why do I write? What do I have to say that hasn't already been said in millions of different ways? Who cares about my body of letters?

I want to cry because the place I covet is a nonplace. I sit in one of the armchairs and put on my dark glasses so no one can see my eyes, puffy as they are with rejection. A man's gaze lights on me and I flinch. He's holding a book by Gilles Deleuze. The Logic of Sense. Is this some new way of flirting that I don't know about? Sitting in a bookstore, holding a book, and making conversation with an astonished-looking girl who has a nice ass? I'm always surprised when men are interested in me. It simultaneously excites and offends me. What if I smile at him? What if we sneak into a corner of the shopping mall? What if we get recorded by security cameras and uploaded to YouTube, and I become an online phenomenon and get asked to pose for Playboy?

I start laughing my strange laugh, half doubled up. He thinks I'm laughing at him. What's so funny, he asks. You are, I say. Me? Why? He's kind of bewildered. If I wanted to give myself to you now, would you go for it? This role reversal shocks him silent. I'll let you lick my cunt if you let me stick my fingers up your ass. All ten of them, one at a time, like in that song, you know? Tommy Thumb, Peter Pointer, Toby Tall, Ruby Ring, and Baby Small. He looks from side to side, afraid that someone might be listening. Toby Tall is my favorite. Which one's yours?

He gets up and leaves. He doesn't even say goodbye. He probably doesn't like having fingers stuck up his ass. I laugh a bit more. And all of a sudden I feel so alone. I sink into the armchair, ashamed. Would you really stick all ten of your fingers up his ass? I jump when I hear the voice. I don't know why, but I hadn't noticed this man. He's balding, with gray hair and thick-rimmed glasses. He's holding the second Harry Potter book on his lap. He looks at me with a welcoming half smile. As if I were a naughty little girl. And not the woman who'd like to whip the bookstore's stallions. I don't know, I eventually reply. And we both laugh.

I like Harry Potter too. I read all the books back to back, eating a tin of condensed milk with a spoon, on the blue sofa in my apartment. I surprise myself with that confession. It's much more than I've said in the whole of the past two days. I haven't read it yet, he says. I'm just flicking through it. But if it's good enough for you to read with condensed milk, then I'll buy the whole series. Did you like the first one? I loved it. The second one, the one you've got there, isn't so good. It's the only one that isn't so good. But the first one is amazing. I don't think much of the films. Have you seen the films? I saw one when I was flipping through the channels one day, but I don't know exactly which it was. I wasn't that keen on it.

That's what I like about living in a city of millions. In a bookstore, in the middle of the afternoon, you can start talking to a stranger about sticking your fingers up his ass and end up talking to another about Harry Potter. I have to go, I say. It was nice talking to you, he says. If you want to do it again, I'm always here on Wednesday afternoons, when I have a break from my clinic. Is he a doctor, a dentist, a psychoanalyst? Here's hoping he's not a psychoanalyst. I smile timidly and leave almost at a run, like a kid. I don't remember to ask his name. Better that way. Names anchor us to an identity. And the best thing about that meeting was that it was fluid, it didn't get printed anywhere. No names, no record.

I've walked halfway back to my apartment when I remember that I don't live there anymore. Thanks to the Harry Potter man, I'd managed to forget my mother. Could he be You-Know-Who? In-joke. When I put the key in the lock and feel the silence of the apartment rushing toward me with its mouth wide open, I want to turn back. But where would I go, now that my foot is caught in the snare? What if I took all my mother's savings and ran away to New York? No, I'd never manage it.

I take off my shoes. My mother isn't a Buddhist, but she's never let anyone enter her house wearing shoes. She thinks that way she can make sure all the dirtiness from the street stays outside. She, who was drowning in shit three days ago. I've only just gone into my room to dump my bag, and I feel invaded. She's been in here. I can feel the memory of her. The smell of her soap. Mom, did you go into my room? I'm furious, and I almost shake her. Laura, I can't even walk. I'm watching Oprah's show, can't you see? I could kill her. Impassive in that bed, with her tentacles moving around the place.

I know she went into my room. Did she read my files? The computer's turned off. Does she even know how to work a computer? It wouldn't surprise me if my mother were as skilled a hacker as Lisbeth Salander. And the sly thing pretends she doesn't even like using a typewriter. And I was almost happy. Bitch. I start to really shake, and I curl up on the bed in a fetal position. Before I dissolve and become just a puddle on the parquet, I open the drawer where I keep my Swiss army knife and walk to her bed. Oprah is interviewing a woman who was sexually abused as a child. And her abuser. Sitting there side by side on the sofa. I roll up my shirtsleeve and open a thin smile above my wrist. I wipe the blood on the TV screen. A Pollock smudge. And we're on familiar ground once more.

17

Laura's locked herself in her room. She's the only one with a key to the door that connects our rooms, I don't have one. Now she's the guardian of all the keys. I prefer it that way. I'm still really tired. She left a bloody mark on the TV. To punish me, I guess. And she is punishing me. I could never get used to her cuts. Every time she cuts herself with that knife, my heart recoils. A few centimeters. That's when I'm sure I love her, because I'm scared of losing her. And, contrary to what she believes, I'm not scared of losing her because I wouldn't have anyone to torment. I just wish she didn't have to cut herself. I know she doesn't go to the beach because her lovely body is a landscape of scars. Small scars that are hard to explain. Or longer, thinner ones. Not like the scars from surgery, which everyone forgives. I don't understand why she does that. And I only let her leave because I was scared that one day the cut would be definitive.

What am I saying? I wouldn't be able to hold her back anymore, even if I wanted to. But I like to think I would. Because Laura, like a hen, never strays far from the yard. She always scratches the dirt near to home, near to me. Laura is a chick that won't grow into a hen. No good even for the cooking pot. Oh God, I shouldn't laugh because it makes my whole body hurt. It's funny that I gave birth to such a weak creature. Maybe weak isn't the word. She left home, left me, and made a life for herself. I kept all her articles. Laura seems good at what she does, and I'd like to give her some praise, but she wouldn't accept it. She might even choose a new career if I told her I liked her work. Perhaps Laura's sentimental rather than weak. In that, she takes after her father. Sometimes I want to say to her: Why don't you just leave, once and for all, go and live your life? But I don't say it. I don't say it because I'm selfish, and Laura is all I've got. For better or worse, I only knew I had a life when I saw Laura carrying her scars around the house.

And I did have a life. And I didn't have a mother. Maybe that's why I haven't been a good mother myself. I never knew what a mother should do. Mine died in childbirth. My birth. I never felt guilty about that. My father didn't blame me either. We were always very rational, he and I. How could I take the blame for the doctors' mistakes when I didn't even know who I was? That was what he used to say to me. And I never questioned him, because I thought it made sense. My father was an attractive man, muscular, in the military. He used to get up long before dawn to do exercises, then take a cold shower. His body was hard all over. No soft bits.

When I turned six, he started getting me out of bed to do exercises with him. Sometimes I wanted to sleep for longer, especially in winter, but I didn't dare ask if I could. And it was worth it, because my father praised me. He said that if all Brazil's soldiers were like me, then the country would be a force to be reckoned with. My father didn't like the way the country was going or the outcome of the war that finished before I was old enough to understand. But we didn't talk about sad things. We had a nice life at home, he and I. And sometimes I thought it was good not to have a mother. And that thought made me feel kind of guilty. But then I decided it was silly, because what I wanted had no bearing on the order of things.

It was a nice life until I learned to read and write. My father taught me himself. When I was a girl, schools weren't mixed, and the daughters of nice families went to convent schools. But my father didn't want me to spend time with other girls, because I might learn bad habits. So I never went to school. He used to give me my first lesson before he went to the barracks, after the exercises and the cold shower. And he would leave me lots of schoolwork to do during the day. I would do it all to perfection, and it kept me pretty busy. Especially the ten pages of handwriting. My writing was rounded, nice and feminine, he used to say.

One night my father started dictating letters to me. First of all, he made me wash my hands with the handmade soap he always bought at the same drugstore because he didn't like the mass-produced stuff that was so popular. He used to say that the dirtiness remained even if you used a whole bar of that stuff in one go. My father's smell was the smell of his soap. And later it would become my smell too.

Maria Lùcia, he used to say, you're my secretary now. I've got arthritis in my fingers, and my handwriting isn't as good or as pretty as yours. You want to be my secretary, don't you? I did want to, of course I did.

Later, I discovered that my father had other women besides me. I was writing to them, crafting each letter with a fine-nibbed gold fountain pen. My father liked tradition, and he liked quality. For him, the past was perfect. And the present, in which girls were increasingly insolent, as he used to say, was no good.

At first they were incredibly refined letters, with words I didn't understand. Osculum, for example. I only understood it the next day, when I disobeyed my father and used the cleaning steps to get the dictionary down from the top shelf. Trembling with fear because it would've been just like him to set some kind of trap to catch me red-handed. Like leaving a black mark on my fingers when I turned the pages, for example. Or poison. No, he didn't want to kill me. Not really. He just wanted to catch me out.

The dictionary was out of bounds for me. In my father's opinion, the dictionary was highly dangerous. And everything that was dangerous had to be eliminated. Or at least tightly controlled. You're an intelligent girl, Maria Lùcia. You take after me. You think you're old enough to have access to all the words in the world? He rounded that aaaaaall in his baritone voice. No, I didn't think I was. But from that day on, I could feel the presence of the dictionary like a third person in the apartment where no one ever visited.

The morning after the first letter, I decided to find out what osculum meant. After my father went out to work, I waited an hour and a half, because sometimes he came back saying he'd forgotten something. But I knew he was checking up to see if I was doing anything wrong. This used to happen several times a week. He

69

would appear suddenly, at some point during the day, with some excuse. He knew that I knew it was an excuse. I knew that I was meant to know it was an excuse. That way he kept constant watch over me, because he didn't trust anyone to be there with me, and I spent every day alone. If there had been cameras back then like there are today, my father would have happily monitored every step I took, and I'm sure he wouldn't even have spared the bathroom.

My father, however, was prudish when it came to my body. He never touched me. Not even to give me a hug or a kiss on my birthday. My father thought a decent relationship between father and daughter didn't include physical contact. And I spent my childhood without any affection, but, because I didn't know what I was missing, I really don't think I missed it. And because I hardly ever left the house, I didn't have much to use as a reference point. And my father was present. Now I know he was omnipresent. So I think I got more affection than any other daughter.

But I'm dwelling too much, like a long-winded old lady.

That morning, I moved the stepladder as carefully as possible so as not to mark the wooden floor and I climbed up to the dictionary. I don't know what weighed more on the way down, the world of words, as my father called it, or my soul. I leafed through the silky pages with the tips of my fingers. L M N O. I found osculum, between osculinflection and oscurantist. The words were burned into my memory. And sometimes, a long time later, when as a grown woman I wanted to forget something terrible, I would repeat them to myself: osculinflection osculum oscurantist osculinflection osculum oscurantist. Even today, I sometimes catch myself doing that. Like when the cat ate part of my foot. My father was right, the dictionary was incomprehensible to me. Of all those words, there was only one I understood. Kiss.

One Saturday, when my father and I were doing our weekly shopping at the grocery store, I saw a young couple with their mouths stuck together in the alleyway behind the store. The guy's hair stuck out at all angles, and the girl was wearing a beautiful wide skirt. I had asked my father if I could play with the puppy that was tied up outside. He let me, so long as I didn't run and get my dress sweaty. I saw the guy with the big hair putting his tongue in the girl's mouth, and she put her tongue in his. At first I stopped dead, watching. Then I felt something warm in my belly and ran after my father. I tugged at his arm, something I never usually did because he thought such behavior improper for a well-educated girl. But I only did it because I thought the girl needed to be saved, and my father could save her. A minute later, I wished I hadn't. My father marched up to them and yanked them apart. It was only a kiss, the girl said, nervously tugging at her skirt. The guy pushed out his chin, but the girl grabbed his hand, and the two of them ran off. From the other side of the road, the girl shouted: "I hope your daughter becomes a hooker!"

I asked what a hooker was, but my father got really mad. He didn't talk to me for the rest of the week. I added it to the list of words I needed to find in the dictionary. But I didn't have time. When I read the definition of osculum, I remembered the scene. The kiss. So that was the disgusting thing my father wanted to do to the woman he was writing to? Actually, to her backside. I

71

felt warm liquid running down my legs and knew I'd wet myself.

I can hear Laura in the next room. She must have insomnia again. I'm writing with a flashlight under the covers so she won't notice the light. I think I'd better stop now. I don't even know why I'm writing this. It's funny how we mean to write one thing and end up writing another. Maybe that was what happened with my father when he dictated the letters. Maybe that's the explanation.

18

The sun comes in through the slits in the blind. It always comes in, even though people like me don't believe in the sun. I prefer the rain because it doesn't oblige anyone to be happy. But it makes no difference now, I'm not going to get out of bed, anyway. And, contrary to what you might think, I prefer not to get up. I can simply close my eyes and imagine my own personal storm. I had nightmares after I'd been writing. It was a long time since I'd talked about my father. Maybe I'd never talked about him. Whenever Laura asked, I just used to say he was a handsome man, a real man, clean and hard. A strong man. She would look at me, and I don't think she understood, because Laura's father wasn't like that at all. And, like me, Laura didn't know many fathers.

How would everything have been if he hadn't died? In my nightmares, he was naked. And instead of being shocked, I grabbed him with my legs as if they were a scorpion's pincers. And I liked it. I think I must be crazy like Laura says. I woke up sweating and wanting to be sick. But I'd rather write. I take advantage of the fact that Laura sleeps late, compensating for her insomnia or because she'd rather lie there, now she sleeps without me. I think that's how we'll end up, she and I, each in our own bed. Dying without fanfare.

There was no more geography, or history, or math. Just Portuguese. Just language. My father dictated longer and longer letters. And I didn't need the dictionary to understand what they meant anymore. The words burned inside me. How could someone who never left the house alone know that something was wrong? The words burned my fingers and opened channels all over my body, down my legs, scorching my skin wherever they went. And the day I'd opened the dictionary, my personal version of Pandora's box, I started wetting myself. I was never curious to discover if any hope remained.

My father would get mad, and I could sense that he wanted to hit me, but he was scared to touch me with his hands. You dirty girl, what got into you, Maria Lùcia? And I knew that dirty was bad, but it was also good, because in the letters he wanted to do dirty things. So I would pee myself again. And the letter had to be put on hold. He would send me to my room, and I would feel relieved.

But the following day, when I was left at home alone, I would need to wash myself continually, my whole body, so much that my skin turned red and started to peel, I almost ripped it off. The words rolled around inside me and contaminated me. I would cry with fear, but no one was ever there. The words got into my head through his voice and stayed there, repeating themselves incessantly. And one day they were shouting so much, one after another and all at the same time, so many times over, that I hit my head against the wall until I passed out.

When my father came home he found me on the floor, my head bleeding. What happened, he asked. And that time I said it, that time I told him. The words from the letter wouldn't stop shouting in my head. I realized he was shocked, and I'd never seen my father shocked before. But he had to take me to the hospital, and the doctor didn't believe the explanation that I'd fallen head first from the top of the wardrobe, where I'd climbed up to get a winter shirt. The doctor said nothing because of the medals on my father's chest, but my father and I both knew he hadn't believed the story. There would be no lasting damage, he assured us. But it would better if I didn't try to get any more shirts from the top of the wardrobe. And my father understood. And I understood too.

When I went home, weeks went by without lessons. The two of us would sit there, in silence, by the light of the desk lamp. At first I felt relived, then, after the first few nights, I started feeling lonely. My father wouldn't look at me and he seemed sad. He didn't speak, but I knew he was sad. But he wasn't a bad father, I knew that too. I used to see him late at night, that man who was accustomed to giving orders to other men, stirring pans of food like a housewife, cooking my favorite dishes for the lunches I ate without him. Devotedly ironing my dresses, a tea towel between them and the iron so as not to damage the fabric. Those times made me realize just how much my father loved me. And I recognized a fragility that was painful to acknowledge.

It was my fault that he was sad, I knew that. I wanted to write, but I was scared. One night, I couldn't stand it anymore and I took the risk. Dad, I said, I think I can go back to studying. He looked at me, somewhat shocked at first. But then I saw a hidden smile spreading across his square chin. Made more horrible because it showed no teeth. A smile that was also a victory. And I remembered how much he liked winning, even though I never doubted his love for a minute. Are you sure you're feeling better? My throat closed, and the words scratched at my windpipe but were stuck there. I could only nod my head to say yes. And everything went back to normal. That was the normal I knew, after all.

I became different. Maybe as a result of the concussion. I didn't pee myself or hear words shouting in my head anymore. I didn't feel anything anymore. I just wrote, and that didn't have anything to do with me. The words were like stuffed birds. With no flesh inside. Dead words like dead birds. Like a dead girl. And when I was alone during the day, I would just sit and listen to the silence in my head. It was better that way.

Isn't Laura ever going to wake up? Suddenly I want to hear her making sounds. It seems incredible to me that someone like her came out of me, slipped out of me soundlessly. The doctor thought she was dead. Because he slapped her hard, and she didn't react. But the nurse confirmed that she was breathing. Then the doctor thought she might have some kind of mental handicap. He told me that much later, very tactfully, when she opened her eyes without so much as a whimper. But I knew he couldn't be sure. That was when I began to suspect that she was mine. My baby. A dynasty of women destined to live without words.

Laura didn't cry. She never cried as a baby. She just lay there with her little eyes open, looking and looking. Soundlessly.

19

My mother stole my words. I feel her presence in everything, in my skin, in how my body smells, in the body of the letters that I write. That's why the words aren't mine. And what can't be said has become another search for what is beyond words, another impotence. She makes me want to tear out chunks of the wall with my hands, and that's what I try to do until I roll on the floor in a ball of pain. Like the woodlouse that as a kid I used to poke with a stick to watch them curl around themselves. I use to spend hours in front of my chosen victim in the yard, and she would never open up. I could destroy her whole world with one of my fingernails, and I only did it once. Crack. And there was nothing left. That was how life ended. With a crack. And that was more terrifying than the horror movies I watched later, one after another, in order to feel a fear that didn't threaten me.

My broken nails don't calm me down, but they tempt me. The desire to cut myself is as strong as the desire to pee once was. I can resist it for a while, but not forever. My spilled blood is my drug. Bizarre and toxic for others. Not for me. It's life. I'm trying to save myself, even if I have to cut my scars because there's no clean skin left. And one day I'll have a new skin, a body I've carved myself. But I know that the stuff inside me will always smell of soap.

Instead of the penknife, I grab a pen and take a stack of office paper from the printer. This time I need to wound the paper with the pen's hard tip, because in a virtual, therefore borderless, world, it's impossible to type words that don't become bodies. I need borders, and I never understood all that marketing bullshit about a world without limits. For me, freedom has always been linked to the ability to build ever-higher walls.

The day I opened the first smile on my stomach, the victorious pleasure of the cut was immediately followed by excruciating pain. As if someone had shoved two large hands into my body and was pulling my ribs apart. I thought a baby was going to come out of me, a monstrous twin sister like in a story I once heard a classmate tell to a bunch of other kids during recess, loud enough that I could overhear from the corner where I was hiding. When the boy's aunt's cousin went to have her appendix out they found a fetus, which had never developed and had stayed there to that day. The fetus even had teeth, the boy said to the other kids, none of whom would sleep that night. I didn't sleep, at least.

Now I was the one giving birth to a monster. And I didn't want to. It was less frightening if it stayed inside me. My mother wouldn't know about it if it stayed inside me. I curled up on the floor like a woodlouse, fearing the crack that would come from an intimately unknown foot. And I was howling inside, but I kept my jaw clamped shut because I didn't want my mother to know, and the echo that reverberated in my chest was as terrifying as the pain because it didn't sound like me. The hands went on opening me up all night, and I couldn't understand why they didn't just tear me apart once and for all, but I equally didn't want the thing to come out. Was there a way of shoving it back inside me like a secret I would keep to myself forever? I hugged my belly because I thought the monster would come out of there, and the smile gaped open.

That's where it started. My body slit open by literality, like everything in me. But what would come out of there, now that it was done? I wished and feared. The other daughter who hid inside me and who my mother sought out with her animal sense of smell. If I gave her that other daughter, would she let me live outside her?

At some point I fell asleep, exhausted. It still hurt when I woke up, but less so. And blood was running down between my legs. I looked for my twin on the floor, but there was nothing except that thick, almost black blood. I put my fingers in it like an animal and sniffed and licked. And it was warm and tasted different to me. Just then, my mother opened the door and saw me on the floor with my fingers all red. I killed your other daughter again, I wanted to say. Your good daughter. I'm the monster. But I was afraid to speak. Her gaze scanned my body and stopped at my legs. She opened her mouth. Not in a smile, but in a grimace. And she said. So now you're a woman.

The labor, in the end, was mine.

20

———

Days later, hair started growing back on my head. But it wasn't brown anymore, like before, it was red. Not orangey, like so many redheads. Really red. And it wasn't smooth anymore, it was curly. Strong. No one in my family has hair like that, my mother said accusingly. And your father had that thin, mousy brown hair. My mother was puzzled.

I loved my new hair from the very first strand. And I've never let anyone cut it, not even her.

I feel like going back to the bookstore. I want to know whether the Harry Potter man will be there. The man who has a clinic. Words grow weak in me, but perhaps it's not my mother's fault this time. This exposed desire always drains me. It's hard to give each thing a name, and each new word messes everything up. Words aren't easy, at least for me. I always have to shut my legs tight so they don't escape, leaving an emptiness that isn't silence.

21

—

Laura's gone to the bookstore. Again. I can't believe how much that girl likes books. She looked at me distrustfully before she left. I think she sensed I was willing her to go out. She's convinced now that whenever she's out, I'll do something I shouldn't, so she scrutinizes every glance of mine as if I'm a criminal. She's scared to death that I might go into her precious room and read what she's written. That's what I do whenever I can manage to drag myself in there. But I'm losing interest.

   Since I started writing in this notebook, all I've wanted to do is write. If I could, I wouldn't sleep, I wouldn't eat, I wouldn't breathe. I'd simply stay here, writing. Now I finally understand why Laura likes writing so much. I always thought it was a waste of time. I would have rather Laura became a saleswoman over any kind of journalist. I never believed that writing was a decent way to make a living, worse still, writing about other people's lives, like she did until recently. And now I'm here, in bed, writing as if my life depended on it. No, not my life. Laura said that a text is only good if it doesn't use the same words all the time. Existence. I'm writing as if my existence depended on it.

Maybe I didn't used to like writing or anyone who writes because words belonged to my father. I was just a body that he used. My letters got stuck there in the lines of that handwriting book like insects in a web. Who was the spider? Now that I'm old, I've gone sort of crazy, laughing alone at jokes that only I find funny.

It's odd how everything happens, and we always surprise ourselves when the time for surprises has passed. I should be thinking about what comes next. But no. I'm sure I'm going to keep tormenting Laura for a long while yet. Not as a spirit, because I don't believe in that stuff. I used to go to the spiritualist center because I thought it was fun to watch those people talking in other voices. I still do think it's fun. It was better than the soap operas on TV. And I liked the atmosphere, I still do. I did charity work, and they thought I was a good woman. It's good to be a good woman, at least in someone's eyes. It's good to be somewhere that we don't have to be ourselves. Laura always reminds me of who I am. And that I don't like who I am. I didn't like myself even before Laura came out of me.

Christ, I do ramble. I've turned into a boring, repetitive old woman who aches when she laughs. Now I realize that I've never laughed so much. In other words, I was never the kind of person to laugh much. And now I can't stop laughing, and it hurts. But what I was saying is that I'm going to torment Laura for a long time yet because I'm certain I've got plenty of life left in me. I might make it past a hundred. I don't know where I get that idea from, because my mother was fragile, as my father used to say, and she died in childbirth. And my father died suddenly, at forty-four. He looked so handsome in his coffin.

A different man, young and hard. Dead, and I knew he was looking at me.

My father never wanted to appear at the spiritualist center. Maybe I went there so he would appear, and I could reassure myself that he's only in one place. But my father is everywhere. Sometimes I'm here, writing in my notebook, and I feel him watching me. Then I make my handwriting worse, because I know that infuriates him.

He was dictating a letter to me, like he did every night. By then, I was the one who cleaned the house, cooked, washed, and ironed during the day. And he would bring me books that he thought were appropriate for me, but which I never liked much. I preferred doing embroidery. I'd taught myself to embroider, and it was something I could do for hours without getting tired. And I had a lot of hours alone in that dark room while I waited for my father to come home from the barracks. He didn't like me to open the curtains because he said there was always a risk that some nosy neighbor might spy on me with binoculars, even though we were on the fifth floor. He was the only one who spied on me twenty-four hours a day, but I kept quiet.

Early in the morning, when we got up, my father would open all the windows wide to let fresh air in. After that, he would draw the navy blue curtains. If I needed light, there were lamps all over the apartment. That was how I did my embroidery for hours on end. And my father had nothing against embroidery, he thought it was an appropriate pastime for a well-brought-up girl. I embroidered flowers, lots of flowers. And most of them came from my imagination, since I hardly ever left the apartment and, in there, I just saw the same shabby plants. I only went out with my father, and only on the weekends, when we did our shopping at the grocery store and he would take me to get an ice cream. Sometimes he would take me to the cinema when they were showing a movie that was compatible with our moral values, but they didn't often show movies that would contribute anything to an upstanding person, as he used to say. In general, he thought cinema was an improper and somewhat dangerous invention, so I was very surprised when I found a photo of Cyd Charisse in the pocket of his pants when I went to wash them. But I only discovered it was Cyd Charisse when she died and I recognized her from the photos in the paper. I don't know many movies or actresses. I think I'm like my father in that respect. Laura's the one who understands cinema, she's always dreaming something up in that head of hers. But why am I talking about this? I have to go back and find my thread. Getting old is disgraceful. It's a good job my father died young, he would have hated it.

The point is that I don't know where those strangely shaped colored flowers came from. My father didn't know either. He looked curiously at my embroidery and never wanted to use any of my towels or quilts at home. We still used the ones from my mother's hope chest. I didn't mind because I was happy as anything embroidering those flowers. They piled up in a room no one used, a room that would have been for my brother, the brother I never had because my mother died having me.

I think I'm repeating myself. As if now I'm the one getting stuck in the web of words. I suddenly feel like I miss those flowers. I stopped doing embroidery when I married Laura's father, I don't really know why. I didn't feel like it anymore, I guess. And I've never wanted to do embroidery again. Until today. Could I still manage? I look at my hands, arthritic like my father's, and notice that they're yellow. How funny, I look like I've got hepatitis. I take so many tablets every day, which Laura gives me meticulously, like everything she does, that it could be a side effect. I've got more chemicals in me than a pack of instant noodles. I'm laughing again. When laughing didn't cause me physical pain, I didn't laugh. I'm reduced now to a stupid old woman.

I was sitting at the varnished table in the den wearing the blue dress that my father liked so much. He was dictating a letter to me. I never forgot the word. It was new and it made me burn inside. He'd just pronounced that word when he opened his eyes wide and lifted both hands to his chest. He repeated the word again in a voice that didn't sound like his. And he fell onto the diamond-patterned carpet. He fell all of a sudden, but for me it was like in slow motion at the movies. I didn't stir. I don't think I moved for a really long time. I carefully put the pen down on the table and called out, slowly. Father. And again, Father. I touched him hesitantly, because my father didn't like to be touched. Nothing. I didn't know what to do. I stayed there, sitting on the floor next to him, maybe for hours. Yes, it must have been hours, because the next thing I knew the sun was shining through the blue curtains. I'd spent the whole night rocking back and forth.

Father? Nothing. What do I do? I wasn't allowed to talk to anyone or open the apartment door when I was alone. And when I wasn't alone, it was my father who talked to the doorman and sorted out whatever needed doing. No one in the building had even tried to talk to me, they must have thought I was mentally handicapped or something. But I knew that there was a doorman on the ground floor. My father would be furious with me if he woke up. But my father was cold now and even harder. And I thought he was dead. How could I know that? I think people have instincts, like animals, even someone who never leaves her apartment. I took the stairs down because I was scared to ride the elevator alone. I stopped in front of the doorman and said, My dad's not waking up. Something like that. He didn't reply straightaway. Or it seemed he took a while. Then, he asked something, but I didn't understand. I stood in front of the reception counter, rocking back and forth.

The doorman went back up with me. I don't remember that, but I know it happened because he was already in the den, standing over my father's body. I wanted to tell him that my father didn't like to be touched, much less by strangers, but my voice was still stuck. Later, it was all a whirlwind. I only remember certain details. My father was dead. Heart attack, they said. Someone came from the barracks and took care of everything. And of me. She's in shock, I heard some woman whisper. Because I was still rocking back and forth. How could they know that I knew nothing? It was the first time we'd received visitors.

I came to when they showed me my father all dressed up in his coffin. He looked so handsome in his full-dress uniform, with medals all over his chest. As though he might wake up any moment and carry on dictating the letter to me. I went into the room belonging to the brother I never had, and picked up the most colorful quilt of all. I covered my father with it, covered his uniform, his medals, his shiny boots, everything. I'm not sure your father would like it, said someone or other's secretary. He always used to say that, when he died, he wanted to be buried with this quilt, I lied. I wasn't so very innocent, after all. I could be bad. Really bad, I think. He was buried with the garish colors and exotic shapes of my flowers. Who knows, they might have germinated, fed by my father's flesh.

From then on, I started paying attention to everything. And when, after the funeral, they asked if I had any other relatives, I said I'd arranged to stay a while with an aunt on my mother's side. No, they needn't worry, the apartment was quite safe. Yes, before I went, I'd open an account in my name so I could receive my father's pension. I was twenty-two, there was nothing they could do. And no one wanted to change the course of his or her own life to look after an orphan my age.

When everyone had left, I cleaned the whole apartment. I scrubbed everything until the skin on my hands started to peel. Then I looked at the handwriting books. And I burned them, one by one, in the kitchen sink. I never wrote the last word he dictated. I'm going to write it now, for the first time. And the word burns me like it did that last night of his life, as if I were still a silly young thing. It's been hovering over us for half a century, and now I'm going to write it. The word that stopped my father's heart. Slowly, because this feels like an important moment.

22

Maelstrom

23

If it didn't seem heretical to describe her as such, I'd say my mother is happy. All of a sudden, she's laughing to herself in bed. She can hardly contain her happiness when I go to the bookstore. No, not hardly. She can't contain it. I have no idea what's going on inside her head, but I know what's going on in mine. I want to see the Harry Potter man again. It's strange, because he's an older man. And I like young, firm-fleshed men. I like to feel muscles moving under my hands, young skin that hasn't yet been chewed up by time. I chew the only virginity that excites me.

I want to set things right. So I plant myself in front of him. With my red hair flaming around my head, I'm a saint from hell. You came, he said finally. And he's got a Harry Potter book in his hand again. The first one, this time. Is the Harry Potter book a lure of yours? A trick to get girls to fuck you? He seems not to notice my bad manners. I was waiting for you. And I thought maybe you wouldn't remember me. So I sat here with this book, as if it were a red rose, because I knew you wouldn't forget about Harry Potter. I don't know. Maybe you're a pedophile. He laughs a good laugh, as if I'd said something nice.

Would you like a coffee? he asks. No, I want to fuck you. He laughs again. He really seems to be enjoying himself. I'm not ready to be fucked yet. Maybe after a few Wednesdays and a few coffees. Are you gay? I ask. And I know the question offends my intelligence. And his. Suggesting that a man is gay because he doesn't want me is undeniably ridiculous. But he forgives me. Gay? Not so far. Once or twice back in college, if I'm honest. He seems infinitely patient. So I finally give in and have a coffee. But I don't know what to say. And this disconcerts me. He doesn't bother to make much conversation. We drink our coffees in silence.

Are you a doctor? I have to ask. No. Dentist? No. You're not going to tell me you're a psychoanalyst! No. I'm a masseur. I wasn't expecting that. Why? I say aggressively. I like touching people. Not me, I don't like it. It would gross me out to touch strangers all over. I look at his hands. Strong hands, which don't match the rest of him. Nice hands too. Well-cut nails. Do you get your nails done? No. That's good, I think it's ridiculous when men get manicures. Why? he asks. It's too feminine.

It's awful, I'm acting like an idiot. I'm here talking to a masseur, and I can't manage to say a single intelligent thing. Sorry, I don't think I should be here talking to you, I'm saying stupid stuff. People always say stupid stuff, I know you're not stupid. The way he stirs his coffee so calmly irritates me. As if he was doing something really important. I already finished mine. And I order another.

And you, what do you do, since we're on the subject? I'm a journalist. Or I was. Now I care for my mother. And I'm trying to write a book. That's it, I said too much. Again. A book? And what's your book about? I don't know. I'm just writing. Or trying to write. I always figured I should write a book one day, that I had something to say. But now I've got my doubts. Doubts? He sounds like a psychoanalyst. Is he going to repeat the last word of every sentence I say? Yes, doubts. I don't think I've got anything to say that hasn't already been said. And I've discovered that I can't even write that well. I'm incapable of inventing anything new, you know. Like in Harry Potter, for example, J. K. Rowling invented a whole world. I can't invent a single word. I'm still trapped inside myself, you know. I know. But maybe it doesn't matter. I think you should just write. Maybe newness doesn't exist. Maybe that's it, a book to show that nothing new exists. That everything is old. And it doesn't do any harm. We're here and that's enough. You're writing and that's enough.

I want to cry. I'm actually talking to someone. You seem too intelligent to be a masseur. Didn't you consider doing anything else? I snap. Writing this sentence down on paper and making it permanent, it seems so predictable. As if it wasn't enough, I'm also a walking cliché. I did a few other things, he says. But I like touching people. You have to be intelligent to know what to do with your hands. I don't like hands. But your hands are nice. I look at my mother-ish hands. I'd cut them off if there were prostheses good enough. He goes to take my hand, but I flinch and knock over my coffee. I don't like to be touched. But you wanted to fuck me. Exactly. I'd fuck you. And I'd tie your hands so you wouldn't be able to touch me. I can touch with my feet too. Then I'd tie your feet. I can touch with my tongue. Then I'd cut out your tongue. And at that moment, I realize I really would cut it out. So does he.

He gets up. Not quickly. As if it were a casual gesture. If you change your mind, I'll still be here every Wednesday.

We can just have coffee. And talk. And one day, perhaps, you might let me touch you. Or not. I'd like to touch you. And to be touched by you. But, if that day never comes, we can just talk. I like talking to you as well. Maybe next time we can share some chocolate cake.

He smiles breezily. And he leaves with his Harry Potter.

I sit there for almost an hour longer. Really unhappy. Suddenly nothing makes sense. But not in the usual way. For a moment, I don't recognize the things around me. It's all strange, as if I've never seen these objects that surround me and I don't know what they are. There's no meaning in what I see. I feel disconnected from myself. And even my hands aren't saying anything that bothers me. Am I having a psychotic episode? I feel something warm between my legs and discover that I peed myself. How embarrassing, my god, how embarrassing. Did anyone see? Luckily, I always carry a coat because I really feel the cold and I hate being cold. I grab the coat from the chair and tie it around my waist. I walk out quickly, I want to run. But running would give me away. I walk back to my mother's apartment.

I go upstairs and peel my clothes off in the kitchen. I put everything in the washing machine and press the button. That's it. It's all over. Laura, I hear my mother's voice. Is that you? Who else is it going to be, Mom? Are you waiting for a boyfriend? My mother never had a boyfriend, not that I knew of, at least. I take a bath for almost an hour. It isn't until I'm done bathing that I go to see her. Is everything OK? she asks. Everything's great with me. And with you? Great too.

We're great.

24

Laura looked really strange when she came home from the bookstore. And she smelled of urine. She thinks she can fool me. All the soap in the world can't mask the smell of her body. My daughter peed herself like a little girl. What could have happened? She's never going to tell me. Between us, truths have never become words. But truths hang between us, in the air we both breathe, in what can't be said, in the things we sometimes do to avoid saying anything. It's better that way. I'm too old for that kind of truth. After feigning silence my whole life, it would be more than I could manage to suddenly start talking.

To talk, I'd have to love better. And I'm not that good at love. When Laura shoots me a look that accuses me of being unloving, she's not that far off the mark. I love her more than I've ever loved anyone, more even than I loved my father, but I think my love is weak. I don't dwell on my grown-up daughter having peed herself but still saying she's great. I'm not great either. That's how it is. Always swearing blind. That's funny. Always swearing blind. Onward, my father would say, the medals on his chest shining so much they blinded me.

What interests me now is telling my story. Not hers. Mine, now I've discovered that words give me a kind of pleasure.

When the apartment emptied of people and my father's coffin was removed, I was alone for the first time. Truly alone. I felt euphorically happy. I opened all the windows and bounced on the sofa like a madwoman, not caring if the neighbors saw me. But no one watched from their window, and when it got dark, I started to worry. My body seemed to belong to someone else. I didn't know where it started or ended. I curled up around myself and stayed there, on the diamond-patterned carpet in the room where my father had been felled by a word. And now that I could open any door, I didn't even want to grab the dictionary.

When the sun came in through all the windows the next morning, I woke up not knowing if I'd slept. I dragged myself to the kitchen, actually dragged myself because I was scared to get up, and I stretched out my arm to take a banana from the fruit bowl on top of the counter. I didn't mind that it was black, I couldn't taste what was on my tongue because it didn't taste of me.

I'd wanted to be free to go out alone, but now I had a fear that was bigger than anything I'd ever felt, bigger even than my fear of the words I wrote in the handwriting book inside me. I could only summon the courage to get up and close the curtains. And I curled up on the floor again in a timeless time, in a bodiless body.

I jumped, then started to shake all over when the sound of the doorbell shot through me. Somebody wanted to come in. And it wasn't my father. My father wouldn't ring the bell. The person rang again, and I started to cry. I was so afraid that I wished I could die. I heard a soft male voice calling me. It took me a while to work out that it was the doorman, the imageless voice of the doorman. I thought I could open the door for the doorman. I opened it. And I stood there hugging myself in front of the open door. Rocking backward and forward.

I came to check if you were OK. I couldn't say anything, there was a padlock in my throat. Do you need anything, have you eaten? I was mute. Can I come in? I nodded. And he came in like a vampire from the movies Laura used to watch endlessly, much later, when all that was over. I'd invited him in.

Only when the door closed behind him did I realize that I shouldn't have invited him in. What would my father think? But my father could only watch me now, his words couldn't reach me anymore. The doorman was small. Thin, with wispy hair, how old was he? He looked like a little rat. A little gray rat. Who's down in the lobby, I thought. But I didn't ask.

He held out a closed hand to me. I didn't understand. For you, he said. And he opened his palm to reveal a coconut candy wrapped in cellophane. I snatched it, like a hungry stray dog on the street that bites the person who pets it, but knows that's not a nice thing to do. I discovered I was really hungry. He settled me onto the sofa and said he'd make something to eat. From the corner of the sofa, I watched him stirring pans of food in the kitchen, my father's pans. Half an hour later, he served me potato and mincemeat stew. Is it good? It was. But I just nodded. When I finished, he led me to my bed, took off my shoes, and covered me with one of my embroidered quilts. I'll come back tomorrow. I'll buy a few things for you.

The next day, he came back with groceries. And the day after that. Aren't they going to miss you downstairs, was the first thing I said. No, I quit. Now I just come here to visit you. I'm working near here during the day. I didn't understand then, but even if I had, I'm not sure I would have done anything. He was a stranger, but that stranger was now the person closest to me.

That was how it happened, out of fear. That little man brought my groceries, and the day I got the pension money, he would take me to the bank. When he wasn't there, I followed my familiar routine. Even though I often felt like my father would catch me doing something wrong, he never appeared. Then I remembered he was dead. Dead, but present. Looking at me suddenly, at random times during the day, ever present. What must he have thought of the half-man who now lived in his place? I enjoyed tormenting my father. And one day I took off all my clothes and danced around naked with the curtains open. Then I rolled up in the quilt from my mother's hope chest and cried for hours, embarrassed that my father had seen me naked. And that for a moment I'd been happy that he'd seen me.

The gray little man took up hardly any space. He didn't talk or ask for anything. There wasn't a handwriting book, because I'd burned them all. I didn't even know if he could read and write. What did he want? I could sense that he wanted something, and, when he was there, I wanted him to leave. But, when he left, I wanted him to come back. One morning, after he left, I got dressed as if I was going out for a walk with my father. I took the elevator. My father used to let me press the elevator button, so I knew where I had to go.

I trembled as I walked past the doorman who was there that day, scared that he would turn me in.

I moved cautiously along the sidewalk. The sun was out, and it made my nipples hard. People looked at me as if something was up, but they carried on their way. And I walked in a straight line, paying attention when I had to cross the street. Pretending to be distracted while I waited to follow someone across like a blind woman who could see, but couldn't make things out. I don't know where I walked to, but it got dark. Then I reluctantly turned around and started walking back. I wanted to keep going in a straight line forever. Without ever stopping. But I was scared of the night. I don't know at what point I started to feel afraid. Then I started to run and didn't care if the cars almost hit me. I didn't hear the horns or the angry shouts. When I got home he was waiting for me at the door. Worried at first, then furious.

I felt like I'd done something really wrong. Then, straightaway, I hated him. You're not my father, I said. That time I said it. No, I'm not. I'm your husband. My what? I didn't understand. Then he said. Be quiet. And he started to take off my dress. I was bigger than him, but my fear was bigger than me. I did what I'd learned to do. I let it happen.

He touched my body carefully, almost fearfully. And he went on touching and touching me in places my father never touched. And I didn't know what he was doing, but I knew he shouldn't be doing it. I couldn't move. Maybe I didn't want to. I wasn't even there. But in some way I was, because I started to like and hate that contact. It was the first time someone had touched me. And it was good and it was terrible.

He started to take off his clothes, and he had a soft, white body, very different than my father's. I was disgusted by that soft, white body, so different than my father's. But I stayed still until he opened my legs, and I felt such great pain that my scream must have woken up all the neighbors. But like everything with me, it was a silent scream, because no one came. He made a muffled noise then rolled on the ground. A few minutes later, he started cleaning me up. And that was how we became husband and wife. But I only knew it was a marriage much later, when I started to go out alone and observe things. By then it was too late to worry about it, and, anyway, I didn't know how to change it.

He wasn't an awful man. Just doing that thing was awful. He carried on working and brought home his own salary, so he wasn't staying with me just for an easy life. I only asked once. Why me? He looked at me with doe's eyes, and I only then noticed that he had nice eyes. Because someone had to look after you. And I wanted to look after someone. That can't have been the whole truth. But it was the truth that could be articulated.

I didn't like it when he touched me. It didn't hurt like before, but I always felt something strange. Afterward, he would clean me up, treating me with what must have been affection. It made me hate him more. Not because he'd done it, but because the strange thing stayed with me for days, and I would want to scrub my legs. I used to scrub my legs when he was at work, and one day I put my hand in that place. And then I thought I was going to die and I passed out. When I woke up, I was still alone on the diamond-patterned carpet in the den. After that I wanted to do it all the time. And when I did, I started to think about my father's words. And after I finished, I was ashamed. When he came home, I would cry until I was gasping for breath. He would ask what had happened, but I wouldn't say anything. But when he went out, I would touch myself and remember my father's words without meaning to. And when I finished, I would be more ashamed. And when he came back, I would cry even more. And one day I said: osculinflection oscurantist. And he cried too.

That Sunday, he took me to the park. And I could see other couples like us on the grass. They were kissing, we weren't. They were cuddling, we weren't. When we got back, I hugged him, and we did the thing that I only learned the name of much later. That was the only time I wanted to do it with him. Because the next day, I vomited. And he knew I was pregnant. I didn't even understand what pregnancy was. I'd always felt as if there was something awful inside me, and now it was growing. That was all I knew. He said it was a baby, that it was a good thing, our child. But how could he know? Only I could.

When my belly started to show, he decided that we needed to move. Since he'd moved into my apartment, we knew the neighbors talked about us. But we weren't bothering anyone, and, back when my father was alive, I never had anything do with them. My father didn't like me replying when other people in the building said hello, so I wasn't very popular. But my pregnancy worried the little gray man. And, one day, he rented a moving van and took me and everything else out of the apartment, and we went to live in a house on a corner in a distant suburb.

That was where Laura was born. But not yet.

That's enough. I haven't enjoyed writing this time. It hasn't done me any good. And my hands are getting more and more yellow. I was really stupid, that's true. I see myself through the eyes of the little gray rat, and I even think I was lucky because I was such a freak. I'm not saying that in a bid for sympathy. I can't stand anyone feeling sorry for me and I don't think anyone ever has. Maybe he did. In the end, I did what I could. Like everyone does. I don't think I was any less normal than anyone else. It's just that I was never very good at disguising the bad smell. I'm lousy at that stuff. Laura learned early on. You just have to not attract attention. You just have to say that your mother, who's rotting in her own feces, had a heart attack. She thinks I don't know, but I do. Neither of us kids herself about sunny mornings, we at least have that in common. But that's enough. I want to sleep without words

25

My mother's scream wakes me in the middle of the night. She's upset. I don't think I've ever seen her like this. What happened, Mom? Are you in pain? Yes, I'm in pain, she laughs manically. You should ask me if I'm not in pain, maybe that's what's making me scream. Oh, great. Now she's going to lose her only virtue, not feeling sorry for herself. Can I do anything for you? Do you want a glass of water, something to help you sleep or for the pain? I want to say that I hated your father. Fuck, newsflash. Thanks for the update. He wasn't who you thought. You always thought he was much better than me. But he wasn't. Right. Got it. Now we can both go back to bed. This was a great conversation. The longest we've had in our entire lives.

She looks at me with hatred. Direct, undisguised hatred. I know she's suffering a lot. A whole life, and this is where we've ended up: My mother is finally starting to lose control. I realize I don't care about her anymore. I don't want to hear her. The story is already written. There's no true time because there's no truth that can't be cut into little pieces of lies. I feel so incredibly tired.

Can you hear the night birds, Laura? Don't you think the night birds' songs are horrifying?

I slam the door. I double lock the door. I get into bed and sleep deeply.

I dream of my father and his soft eyes. I never wanted to hurt you. I swear, he says. And I say, I know. Dad, I know. I know you love me, Dad. I've always known that. I didn't want to hurt her either, your mother I mean. I know, Dad, you couldn't hurt anyone. I was just so lonely. And I wanted someone to be waiting for me at the end of the day. I know, Dad. It's all OK. I don't know how to write, you know. I'm ashamed to say it, but I only know how to write my name, and I learned to read the names of the bus lines. If I could write, I would. But I don't know how to write and I'm scared. I know everything I need to know, Dad. I always knew everything I needed to know about you. Are you alive, Dad? Could we have coffee one of these days? I miss you so much.

It's a good dream. But suddenly one of her nails, my mother's curved, yellow nail tears the dream in half and crushes my father. The claws scratch at my bedroom door, and she shouts my name. I fling the door open, and her body falls onto my feet. Again. I'm in a lot of pain, Laura. Why didn't you open the door? I've been knocking for ages, I think I'm going to pass out. Laura, you have to take me to the hospital.

Laura, you have to save me.

26

Save me. She's paralyzed by those words as she helps her mother into the taxi. It's as if she's been given a shot of Botox somewhere inside her. On the outside, she moves and does what's expected of her. But inside, nothing moves, she's frozen by the words. In the delicate light of the new day, she realizes how yellow her mother's skin is. How could she have failed to notice that? Does she have hepatitis? It doesn't matter. Her mother wasn't asking for anything, she wasn't complaining, she wasn't anything at all. Who's this mother, asking for salvation? Where has this come from?

That same night, her mother loses control and declares her hate for her father, as if she's suddenly turned into one of those vulgar women determined to malign their ex-husbands. Her mother had never said anything like that before. And she suddenly opens up in the middle of the night. And then asks to be saved. And what if she just opened the door and ran away? Now. She's got her wage-guarantee fund saved up, she doesn't need her mother's money. She slams the taxi door and runs. She gives the taxi driver the address of the hospital and disappears into the crowd. Then, new name, new woman, new life. Free from her mother, the past, the present, the future. From nothing. To nothing. From nothing to whatever she wants.

Did you know that most people who disappear don't want to be found, Mom? Her mother barely lifts her yellow eyes. She knows she'll be all right there. Her mother is in pain. She looks at her mother. She can touch her mother's pain. What's going on with her mother? What's her mother cooking up now? She's scared. She's not sure if she's scared of her mother, or for her.

They remain in silence until they reach the emergency room lobby. They'll have to wait hours there, she's sure of that as she looks around. People are lined up, each one closed inside a pain that has become their everything. All that matters is that pain, like the pain felt by the mother at her side, her yellow fists clenched, closed as if she's going to punch someone. A few people bleed from old wounds, a child cries. Only those accompanying them are talking nonstop as if at a self-help group. But no one leads the group, and they all clamor to give their testimonies at once. No one wants to listen, they all need to speak. They talk about pain and urine and blood and feces. She doesn't want to listen. And how selfless they are for caring. The string of disclaimers is so long, resentment rears its head in every phrase. They talk as if their sick companions weren't listening. She doesn't want to hear them, but she can't help it. She starts to feel suffocated, she wants to run out and leave her mother there. Mom, you're going to have to pay for private treatment if you don't want to spend all day here. I've got money in the bank, her mother says. I know. I'll go and talk to the receptionist.

They immediately change worlds. Now they're waiting in a room with newly painted walls and air-conditioning, with designer armchairs and fancy glass vases. Then her mother is called in, and she goes with her. She recounts her mother's recent history, and the doctor finds the file. The doctor frowns, but composes herself again. We're going to have to do a range of tests. I don't think it's your kidneys this time. It would be best if you could stay here. For a day or two, just while we do the tests. It'll be easier and quicker if you stay here.

She fills in the paperwork and goes home to get her mother's pajamas and toothbrush. Her soap. She's still got Botox inside her. If she tries to cut herself, will the knife get stuck in her paralyzed soul? She wants to find out. She plays with the knife in her hands. She draws it lightly over her skin, between her breasts. And it turns her on. She starts masturbating with the knife moving between her breasts. She opens her cunt with the tip of the knife, but only puts her fingers in. She turns the knife around and shoves the handle in, hard. A few streaks of blood run down from the hand that's holding the blade. But it's only. She comes.

She washes her hands thoroughly with her mother's soap. She lathers her cunt with her mother's soap. And she likes it. She enjoys the thought that she raped herself. She'd like the Harry Potter man to see her now. No. A minute ago. When she was shoving the handle of the knife into her cunt over and over. She comes again. Picturing the Harry Potter man's gaze. Women's magazines could interview her about tips for always having multiple orgasms. Take a really sharp knife. It could be the one you use to carve your family's Sunday roast. And slowly slip it into your vagina. Laugh until you cry.

Then, go to the hospital.

27

The black-feathered-doctor is there when she enters her mother's room. I'm taking charge of your mother's care because I already know her case history, she says. As if she was about to question her presence. She's not interested in tests of strength, hasn't been for a long while. But for some reason, the doctor irritates her. She wants to hurt her. Good afternoon. And she says the doctor's first name. How are you? Polite and superior. What was that you said, Adriana? The doctor is disconcerted. Good afternoon. I was just explaining that I'm taking charge of your mother for the time being. Taking charge of my mother, she wants to say. Then take her home with you. Could you come to my office for a moment to sign some paperwork?

No. Her mother's voice. Say what you have to say here. Her mother's tone is harsh. What's going on with her mother? Suddenly so full of human emotions? The doctor is just asking me to go to her office to sign the paperwork. It's routine, Mom. No, the doctor wants to talk to you about my illness. Say it here, in front of me.

She thinks the doctor is going to take off. Her feathers ruffle, her beaky nose sticks forward. But the doctor belongs to a flightless species and only takes a few faltering, aimless steps around the room before running her hand over her coat to smooth a nonexistent crease and then leaning on the bed. It's fine. If that's what you prefer, Maria Lúcia.

She draws closer and sees her hands grip the bed's guard-rail. She suddenly realizes that she's deaf. I can't hear anything, she wants to say, I can't hear. But she can hear. You've got a hepatoma. A what? Cancer of the liver. We're not sure why there was no sign before, when you were here the first time. But we checked all the tests, and there really wasn't anything. This kind of tumor generally develops very quickly and sometimes there are no symptoms, but something should have shown up a month ago. The fact is that you have a very advanced tumor. It's primary, which is also less common. We'd usually see this in someone with hepatitis B or C or cirrhosis of the liver. It's less common to see a primary liver cancer in someone like yourself, who's not suffering from one of those diseases. And the fact that nothing showed up a month ago means it's quite aggressive. Which is also uncommon because, in general, at your age, tumors tend to develop more slowly.

She knows she's listening to every word. It isn't that she's not listening. But she's at the bottom of the sea, and the sound she hears is muffled. No, she's at the bottom of a swimming pool. No, the bath. Her mother pulled her out by the hair and saved her from the swimming pool. Her mother pulled her out of the bath at the house on the corner when she was drowning. But who had put her there? Mom, who tried to drown me in the bath when I was a baby?

Excuse me? The doctor looks at her as if ready to give her a shot of Valium right in the jugular. The bath, someone tried to drown me in the bath when I was little. Laura, let the doctor carry on explaining the diagnosis. Her mother's voice, perfectly controlled. Pass me the bread knife, Laura, but don't try to open your vein with it before I can cut a slice. The doctor clears her throat. She seems almost happy. It's strange how people feel good when someone else's craziness is noisier than theirs. The doctor is in control now and can carry on with her white speech. White, she thinks, isn't the sum of all colors, it's the absence of all feelings. White has no pain or fear or villainy. That's why it's the color of peace, because it's the sum that subtracts the human.

As I was saying, the tumor in your liver is primary, but we've already detected metastases in your lymphatic system, right lung, and stomach. She interrupts. We know this is all pretty uncommon, Adriana, especially the fact that my mother was in the ICU here at this hospital a month ago, and nothing was detected. We want to know what that means. According to the weather forecast, it will be sunny with showers throughout the day in the southeast and in part of the north. What does that mean? She can't stand the tone of this conversation. Adriana, we want to know if my mother is going to die. We're all going to die one day, the doctor says with a condescending little smile. No, she won't allow it. We want to know if my mother is going to die now, of this disease. And not from a stray bullet or a tsunami or a heart attack in her sleep.

The doctor winces and suddenly seems older. The oncologist thinks we should operate as soon as possible. Tomorrow or the day after. Once we've operated, Maria Lúcia, you'll have to regain strength before we start chemotherapy. And what, Adriana, does that mean? If there are metastases, are you going to remove the affected parts of those organs so she can carry on, or what? What are the chances of remission? Yes, she too knows how to use difficult words since writing so many articles about cancer. No, since the advent of Google.

I can assure you that we're going to fight this, Maria Lúcia.

The doctor doesn't look at her. She talks directly to her mother, who looks like a model from Madame Tussauds. The waxy eternalization of the moment when a woman learns she's going to die not one day, but soon. I'm not going to let you carry on hiding behind your professional little speech. What we want to know, Adriana, is if there's any chance she could be cured. Or if this surgery will only serve to make all of you feel less impotent. Is my mother going to die from this disease? Or does she stand a real chance if she undergoes surgery and chemotherapy?

You need to calm down, says the doctor, her hands twisting the stethoscope. I understand that it's a difficult time, but attacking me won't do any good. I'm not God, I can't say whether your mother will die from this disease. My dear Adriana, that is precisely the point. Neither you nor your colleagues are gods to decide whether my mother is going to die painfully, cut open unnecessarily. But there must be sufficient research to indicate whether a woman of seventy, with primary cancer in her liver and metastases in her lymphatic system, stomach, and right lung has some chance of being cured and so should undergo surgery, or if that's just going to worsen her quality of life. With the right information, my mother can at least choose how she's going to live out the final part of her life. Do you understand what your role is in all this? It's not up to you to decide how my mother will live. It's up to her.

She wants to laugh at having referred to quality of life. But she knows her little speech is coherent, modern even. It's a clash of words, for the time being. And words also serve to clothe us. Suddenly she wants to protect her mother from all the misery that the doctor has no way of foreseeing, the misery that those white-coated sub-gods mean to subject her to. Where does this protective instinct come from? So now they're

united, in illness, as they never were in health? Is the relationship between mother and daughter a kind of marriage?

We have the right to know, you see. We want to know
how long my mother has left. And what might happen in each
scenario. It's normal for relatives to feel like they're losing control at a time like this, the doctor says in her unshakeable tone.
But she notices her white shoe tapping the floor. We have a
support group that you could join, and it might be worth you
speaking with the psychologist.

I just want you to answer my questions, Adriana. Could
you give us some answers? I'm going to see if I can find the
oncologist, the doctor says. And she leaves, her shoes ham-
mering the floor. Instead of looking at her mother, she now
looks at her nails. She notices that she broke one when she
grabbed the bed's guardrail. She's losing nails along the way.
Now of all times, when she needs good sharp nails. She feels
her mother's yellow eyes boring into her. She wants to touch
her mother, but can't. She reels with the force of the hatred
that suddenly swells up. Like one of those storms that rips
houses off hillsides. She hates her mother. Could her mother
die suddenly of a heart attack? Without blood, without moans,
without discharge? Without days, months. Pain.

She thinks she ought to touch her mother. But she can't.
It's harder than ever to touch her. Now that her mother's body
is decomposing inside, now that her flesh is degenerating
as well as her soul. Could it be that her soul was so rotten it
infected her flesh? She can smell her mother rotting. No, it's
not her imagination. Her mother stinks like offal left out in the
sun. That's what disease is, after all. Guts being eaten from the
inside, the body betraying and devouring itself. In her mother's
case, the malign cells must have indigestion. That thought's

so funny it makes her burst out laughing. When the oncologist comes in, tears of laughter are rolling down her face.

Sorry, doctor. Yes, she calls him doctor. I think I'm a bit shaken up. He shoots her a hard look. No sympathy. Yes, I've been told you didn't react well to the diagnosis. She quickly recovers from the blow. No, doctor, I reacted very well, in fact. Isn't my reaction in your handbook? What a shame. Her eyes are dry now. They're at the same level as the doctor's glasses. His hair is graying, a bald patch spreads back to the middle of his scalp. She sees nothing there. Nothing in those inexpressive eyes. Not even irritation. A touch of boredom, perhaps? We want answers, that's all, answers that someone as eminent as you, doctor, can surely give us. And she smiles her best toothless smile.

Go ahead, dear. What would you like to know? The doctor changes tack. She doesn't. You're mistaken, doctor, I'm not your dear. I can guarantee that you wouldn't want me as your dear. Another perfect toothless smile. She sees desire flash through the doctor's eyes, moving horizontally. Maybe he would like to call her dear, after all, and rub his Viagra-hard cock in her red cunt.

We'd like to know, doctor, what your name is. Paulo. Dr. Paulo Roberto Simões Lopes Neto. He pronounces the name as if she should know it. His chest puffs up as he says it. He comes at the thought of his own importance. But no, she doesn't recognize a single letter. We want answers, Paulo. Objective answers. No beating about the bush. My mother and I deal better with clear information, even if it's hard to take. For instance, as a starting point. Is there any chance that my mother's cancer could be cured?

The doctor hesitates, but only for a few seconds. If you prefer objectivity, then let's be objective. It's a fairly aggressive tumor and there are already metastases in other organs and the lymphatic system. If you were in the public health system, I couldn't recommend surgery. But since you are in the fortunate position of being able to afford private treatment, my advice is to fight it. We can remove the affected parts of the organs and begin chemotherapy as soon as your mother recovers from surgery. She thinks that perhaps the doctor hates his own mother, which causes a shadow of laughter to pass over her face, disconcerting him. Yes, now the doctor is paying her plenty of attention. She notices when the doctor adjusts one of his few strands of hair.

What are my chances of surviving after that, doctor? Her mother's voice emerges from deep in the bed where she already appears dead. She and the doctor seem surprised that her mother is there. She thinks she won't be able to see her mother alive again, now that she knows she's dying. She's going to look at her and see a corpse, not her mother anymore. The doctor shudders and addresses her mother as if talking to a child. Well, Maria Lúcia. It is Maria Lúcia, isn't it? I don't think it's worth just focusing on statistics. In medicine, we have to fight. To the end. I don't really care what you believe, doctor. It's my life. What are my chances if I do what you suggest?

She feels proud of her mother. She's the mother she knows again. Indifferent to other people's approval. She's alive, after all. The doctor is caught off guard, this isn't the way people talk to him. He shouldn't even be there. This is a conversation for one of his assistants. I can see that you'll be a difficult patient. I haven't decided if I want to be your patient, doctor.

She explodes with pride for her mother. I shouldn't stand for this, but I understand that you're in shock. So here it is, if you prefer the most painful way. Your chances are slim. But what would you rather do? Die without a fight? This way we can at least guarantee that we'll prolong your life. And what life would I have, doctor, after undergoing such a surgery and then chemotherapy?

The doctor doesn't know what to say. He isn't used to being confronted, and he hates the experience. He looks at his Rolex to show that he's losing precious time. In his case, precious isn't a metaphor. Well, there are brave people who fight to the end and don't let themselves be beaten by the disease. Under pressure, the doctor doesn't think twice about hitting below the belt. Her mother won't let herself be brought down. She counters, looking him in the eye. I'm a coward, doctor. If there are no real chances of a cure, I'd rather accept it. All I want from you is a guarantee that I won't be in pain.

You see, Maria Lúcia, I don't have a choice. I have to do everything in my power to save you or I could be sued for neglect. As such, we'll have to perform the surgery, and it will have to be as soon as possible because there's no time to lose. You're not going to touch me. And, if you do, I'm not going to pay you. And then I'll sue you all the same. The doctor snorts. Now she can see the little dots on his scalp from a hair transplant. Paulo, do you take finasteride? she asks. The doctor doesn't get it right away. When he does, he's furious. I'm going to call the psychologist. He slams the door on the way out.

She's happy to look at her mother. Laura, get my things and let's get out of here. But we can't, Mom. Of course we can. Help me up before they grab me and force me to have that operation. It's like a movie. A B-movie, but a movie nonetheless. She puts her mother into a wheelchair. And her heart pounds in her chest as she pushes her through the corridors. She wants to run, but she holds back. She smiles at the men and women in white coats walking the other way. They slip through the wards as if out for a stroll. Out on the street, she hails a taxi. She helps her mother into the backseat and gives the address of her apartment.

The two of them look at one another and laugh like school-girls. They ran away. Then they're embarrassed by their inti-macy and don't say a word until they get home. When she's settling her mother into bed, she says. I'm going to have a bath. Her mother grabs her wrist with a hand identical to hers.

Laura, you have to kill me.

28

———

I plunge into the bathtub where someone once tried to drown me and my mother saved me. It's strange. Here, where I almost died, I feel safe and warm and protected. It's as if the water isn't liquid, it's a wall that keeps me separated from the world. I think I'm like those homeless people who cook and shit and make love in the street, but don't seem to notice that their house doesn't have doors or walls. They create invisible walls and believe in them. I'm sure they believe in them because they move as if they can't be seen. In the bathtub, I can't be seen either, even when my mother scratches at the door. I hum a children's song which describes a house that didn't have a floor or walls.

I remember the whole song. Our bodies, mine and my mother's, are that house with no fixed boundaries. There's a dam in my throat, and Vinicius de Moraes knocks it down. My sobbing is now a river that bursts through dikes and comes rushing down, bringing logs and stones with it.

How does my mother have the courage to ask this of me? When I was fifteen, I wrote this in my school exercise book: Is a mother's death a daughter's life? Is a mother's life a daughter's death? Back then I already knew there wasn't space for both of us in the same life, in the same

body. One of us had to die. And I wanted to live. I used to
tell myself stories in which I killed my mother in the most
horrific ways. Always painfully. Her eyes last, so she could
see what I was doing and how much she was bleeding. While
I tortured my mother, I looked into her eyes so she would
know that she had lost. That I had won. And, last of all,
I would prick her eyeballs with the tip of a knife or burn
them with a cattle prod. I used to dream of a life without my
mother, with a body that was mine alone. Like a life from a
margarine commercial in which I had a different mother,
a different father, and even a brother and a dog. Later on,
I dreamed I didn't have a family at all. I was an adventurer
traveling the world. Sitting on a hotel balcony, I would sip
an exotic cocktail with a cigarette dangling from the corner of my mouth and tap away at a typewriter, occasionally
pausing to look out at an ever-changing, foreign landscape.
I would wear a cynical look, and at night I would sit at the
bar and say in a low, husky voice: Play it again, Sam. In my
dreams I was Humphrey Bogart, not Ingrid Bergman. I was
Hemingway, not Jane Austen. Without a mother, I didn't
need to be a woman. Who would know? I could claim any
body as my own. And I wanted to have a body that didn't
hurt, a smooth, hard body, a body that could thrust into
someone and hurt inside. A body that didn't bleed with
every dead ovum, every live child.

Once I got a bit older, I knew I wouldn't be brave
enough to kill her and stopped inventing assassinations.
Instead, I used to imagine that she would die from some
disease and I would become free. But she does not even get
sick, my mother, bad people are always in good health. I was
sure she'd outlive me and would carry me, bound to her
body. I would be like one of those arms that atrophies and

hangs beside a person's body, dead, with no muscle tone or movement. Or I would be my mother's phantom limb, which would throb on stormy nights and winter days. Yes, my mother would live forever, and I was done for.

Back then, I used to bleed myself more. And once, just once, I cut my left wrist with the aim not of separating myself from it, as usual, but of dying. I didn't have the courage to go through with it and took myself to the hospital. I knew then that I really wanted to live. I don't know why, but I wanted to. And now she's asking me to kill her. Before that she asked me to save her.

And now that I'm authorized to kill her, I feel like this is her greatest revenge, not mine. She wants me to carry her death in my soul so I can never be free of her body. So that, instead of a corpse, she might live forever in my guilt. My adorable mother is asking me to be her murderer. Does she want me to rot in prison for matricide, isolated from the other prisoners because my crime is so heinous that even the worst criminals can't bear it?

What I should do is take her back to the hospital, like a good, concerned daughter. And let the doctors open her up. And let them do whatever their greedy omnipotence and our bank account allow. All the worst things I dreamed up for her, entirely within the law. Sometime later she'll die in pain, alone in the ICU, all sewn up, bald from the chemotherapy, trapped by tubes and wires, unable to talk or reach out to me. And then I'll be free and perfectly integrated into society. That, in the end, is the cruelest way to kill her. And I'll still be a dedicated daughter. For my mother's own good, I sent her to the hospital so she could be saved against her will. I'll fight for her life until the end, by her side, never becoming disheartened. Another operation? Definitely.

There's a new drug we can try? Of course we'll try it. It has painful side effects that haven't been fully identified yet? What a shame, but we need to think of the greater good, which is saving her life. More sessions of chemotherapy? Absolutely, the important thing is to keep fighting. Why don't we try radiotherapy as well?

And I'll stay there, by her side, day and night, so as not to miss a second of her suffering. And the nurses and nursing assistants and the entire medical team and the psychologist and even the social worker who looked at me as if I were a worm will shed tears when they see how dedicated I am. And people will come from other floors and wings of the hospital to accompany me in my devotion. And even Alzira will tell the spirits that the most loved mother in the world will be joining them in heaven. And someone will tell the fireman who, feeling sorry that he judged and disparaged me, will invite me for dinner and then extinguish the blazes in my body with his powerful hose. Shit, that last bit was in such bad taste.

Isn't that the perfect crime? No fingerprints, no leads. Totally within the law and adhering to the highest standards of moral behavior. Yes, I finally have my chance. And that's precisely what I'll do tomorrow. Let my mother sleep peacefully in her own bed for the last time. She can count on my love.

29

I'm scared. And at the same time, I'm kind of happy. I guess this is the happiness I've heard so much about. I'm dying and I want to jump. I want to bounce on the sofa, like I did when my father died. Did I tell you about that? I jumped on the sofa until I almost passed out, with the windows open wide. I don't think I've ever been so happy as the moment Laura and I looked at each another in the backseat of the taxi, like two friends who'd pulled some trick. I never had a friend, at least not with whom to share that kind of complicity. And I don't think I'd ever felt Laura's love before. Not in that way. I thought we could run through the streets, and eat ice cream, and smear ice cream on our school skirts. I always wanted to have a school uniform, with a pleated skirt and bobby socks. I think Laura always wanted a mother like Maria von Trapp in The Sound of Music. She loved that film, she watched it millions of times. But, when I think about it now, I don't believe I ever wanted to be a mother, not Laura's or anyone else's. I wanted to be the daughter of a huge family who would pay me lots of attention or tell me to write in my handwriting book. A family whose father would come home from work with a distant look in his eye and ruffle our hair affectionately. And that was all. Sort of like in that silly film, just without running away to Austria. In that life, Laura could be my younger sister, and we'd get on well. We'd break rules together and cover each other's backs when someone wanted to hurt us, or if our father found us out. In a life like that, I think I might even be able to sing. And Laura would make a great sister, I'm sure of it. But now I'm going to die. I say that to myself, but it's like I don't understand it. It's not as if I'm that keen on living, anyway, but I don't want to die. I always thought I'd go like my father, just drop dead one day. And I wouldn't even have to know about it. And now my body is betraying me so miserably. Because that's what there is. There's an enemy attacking me from inside. It's as if the cat's inside me now, digging his claws into my liver, my lung, chewing my stomach. I don't want this body. It doesn't belong to me anymore. I'm going to pretend this body isn't mine. And really it isn't. It never was. That's it. I don't have a body and I'm not going to die. Like Alzira says, it's just a covering. A case for my soul. But I don't believe that, I'd like to believe it but I can't. I used to listen to those embodied spirits at the center and just thought it was funny. That different way of speaking, as if the dead change their accent when they enter the hereafter. I don't think I've got any kind of soul. If I do, my flesh is all mixed up with it and isn't going to let it go without tearing off a chunk. These tumors that are killing me feel like part of me as well. It's odd, because I know where they are, the tumors. If I were brave enough, I think I could even poke them. Those things that have got me surrounded on the inside. I want to tear myself out of me, like Laura does with her penknife.

She's never told me why she likes bleeding all over the place. I can't bear this agony. I need Laura to kill me right now. It'll be quick, like dropping dead all of a sudden. But I didn't think Laura would have the guts to do it, she's always been so cowardly. But deep down maybe she'd enjoy killing me. Laura kids herself that I'm the fire-breathing dragon standing between her and freedom. My daughter's so silly. I'm mad at her now. Because she's going to live, and I'm not. No, I wouldn't give my life for Laura's, I have to say that. I'm not that kind of mother. I don't even believe that kind of mother exists. Only in soap operas and the kind of sentimental movies that win Oscars. I'm mad about everything she's going to experience once I've gone. I want to stay and scratch Laura's door so she never forgets the sound of my nails. It's so much fun to scare her. How is it possible to love and hate at the same time? That's what I feel for Laura, a love that hates and a hate that loves. I'm scared of pain, of dying a painful death. I'm going to ask Laura to kill me now. Is it so wrong to ask your daughter to do that? Some might think it strange. But I don't care. I think death has made me more selfish. I don't care about anything except the cat that's eating me from inside. That's all I think about, that there's a cat gnawing at me. But no greedy doctor is going to open me up and pretend to save me. I know that the animal's claws have reached every part of me, and they've dug deep in some places, I can feel it. If he dies, he'll take me with him. But I'm going to kill him before he destroys me entirely and poops me out. I don't want to become cat feces. Or better still, Laura will kill me. After all, she owes me her life. Laura can complain all she likes, but she was born of my body. Like

a cancer. That was what I thought she was. Did I already
tell you that? I want to tell you. One of the times when
the gray little rat shoved himself into me, I got pregnant.
But I didn't know what that meant. The little man seemed
happy. And I was horrified to see my belly growing,
stretching my skin. I had a creature inside me, just like
now. It's the same feeling. Get this thing out of me, I
shouted. But the little man would just look at me with
those sad eyes of his. It's a child, you're going to have a
child. A healthy baby for us to love. I didn't understand.
How could I? One day that thing tore me apart and came
out of me. At home, because the little rat was scared of
something, I don't know what. It was the same pain as now,
the very same. I remember feeling surprised to be alive
when it was over. I looked at the bloody little monster and
was so disgusted. It was another little rat. I saw that it
had one of those things between its legs that one day it
would try to shove into me like its father did. Monster
Jr. crawled onto my body and wanted to suck my breasts.
Monster Sr. said I had to let it, but I wouldn't. No chance.
That thing had already sucked at my insides for an
eternity, and, now that it was out, it wanted to suck
the outside of me. I screamed that I would throw it at the
wall if he didn't get it off me. And the little man had the
nerve to look at me with undisguised hatred. When he
went out to work, and I had the strength to drag myself
along, I took the lump of flesh and drowned it in the toilet.
Yes, I really did it. And I never felt sorry about it. I only
discovered that I wasn't to blame when I read one of
Laura's articles on post-natal depression. I didn't care.
I never felt guilty. I did it three more times. When my
belly started to grow, I would beg him to get that thing

out of me, but he always pretended not to hear. And he had to leave the house sooner or later. And that was that, it was all over. I buried the last one myself, in the yard. Each time, when he came home, he planted a tree on top of each one, to mark the spot. As if that would absolve him of the crime of having put the thing inside me. A yellow ipê, a bougainvillea, a purple glory tree, and a lime tree. Those limes were sweet, but the fool never drank my limeade. One day Laura came along. I'd stopped even caring. My belly would grow, the thing inside would feed off me, it would split me open when it came out, and then I would drown it in the toilet. The idiot would bury it in the yard and plant a tree. Because I never left the house, the neighbors couldn't even have known that I was pregnant. They were perfect crimes, even though for me it never felt like a crime. If I begot the thing, even by force, then it was mine to destroy. I was always sure of that. That was what I used to say to the little man at the start, when his little eyes were boring into me as if I were the greatest disappointment in the universe. Him of all people, who must still have thought the Earth was flat. Afterward, I didn't even bother to say anything. If he didn't want that to happen, all he had to do was not shove himself into me at night. I'd already learned the relationship between cause and effect, without anyone ever explaining it to me. Then Laura came along. Although I didn't know it was Laura. I spent the whole pregnancy pretending I didn't notice my belly. But when it was time for her to be born, she wouldn't come out. I started to get breathless and turn purple. The gray little rat had to take me to the hospital. And that was where Laura was born without making a single sound. When we got home, the little man said that if I killed her, I'd be arrested, because she'd been registered. During that pregnancy, I'd gone out because I'd wanted to show myself to people, I don't know why. I wanted them to see me. I wasn't scared of being arrested because I knew I wasn't in the wrong. She was my daughter, wasn't she? I could do what I liked with her. She hadn't grown in his belly or fed off him. When the little man went out to work, begging me not to do anything bad, I took Laura to the toilet to drown her. And when I put her head in the water, she didn't cry like the others. Laura looked at me. She just looked at me. And I have to confess that I felt something different. In some way that little monster knew who I was. And I couldn't do it. I wanted to, but I couldn't. I held her gently and stayed there, on the bathroom floor, rocking back and forth. That was where her father found us. And his happiness almost made me try to drown her again. But I knew I wouldn't be able to. I think it was love, but I only knew the name much later. I'm sure that those women in Laura's magazines who show off their healthy maternal bellies and talk about the wonders of motherhood all have at least one day, just one day, when they feel like there are monsters inside them, eating their way out. I might be the only crazy woman in the world, but I doubt it. I doubt it. It's just that no one has the courage to admit we're living in the age of idiots. I loved Laura, that's the truth. Despite everything. And I saved her from myself out of love. That was what I was doing much later, when I gave her my breast and almost went to jail. I was trying to make up for it. And that's why I didn't like to see her father near her because I knew what might happen when he slinked around the walls like a rat. I didn't want any little rat, gray or any other color, getting into my daughter's bed. But it seems that everything in me is warped, and Laura thinks I'm an aberration. What I want to say is that, just because we don't know how to do things the right way, doesn't mean we don't love. I just didn't know the right way to love, that was all. How could I? No, I'm not asking for forgiveness or compassion. I know very well I wouldn't get it, because it's better to think I'm the only evil one and the rest of humanity is good and pure. But, like it or not, I'm also a child of this world. And everything others did to me or I did to them was done here. That's what I have to say about the past. Now I don't want to write any more about what happened. Yes, Laura, you drowned. Not in a swimming pool or a bathtub, like you seem to believe, and I let you believe because there are some things that shouldn't be clarified. I don't even know how you can remember something that happened in the first days of your life. You're not normal either, Laura. You inherited my deformed genes and remember things you shouldn't. I saved you, but I saved you from myself. I was both your murderer and your savior. And I think that's what all mothers are, to a certain extent. Your Maria von Trapp doesn't exist. She was a stepmother, remember. At some point, the children had killed their real mother. But no one ever wanted to know what happened to her. Maybe the tumors that are doing away with me are the babies I killed, and they've come back for revenge? I'm scared, but if that's what it is, I'm not going to complain, because now they can, and I can't. I'm old and I can't drown anyone anymore. What will death be like? The end, that's it? The end, nothing more? The end, it was just an accident? The end, and I was only a girl who wrote obscene words in a handwriting book, and a woman who killed babies, and a mother who didn't know how to be a mother, and an old woman who started writing again because she was scared of being forgotten or remembered in the wrong way and wanted to leave her version of a story no one cares about? I'm grateful that this notebook doesn't have lines. If I'd known earlier that it was so simple, that there were unruled notebooks where everything fit, I might have had a different life. I think that's it, in the end. I was a mistake. My life was one big misunderstanding. And even if I weren't dying, it would be too late. Is there any life that isn't one big misunderstanding? I didn't know I liked living so much, but I do. I like it now that I'm going to die. You won't be there where I'm going, Laura. I know I'm going somewhere. If heaven and hell exist, I'm probably going to hell. But, dare I say, it'll be an injustice. Because I didn't know. I just didn't know. Can people be condemned for things they're oblivious to? Or is there an asylum in the hereafter for the crazies like me, or for those who are unimpeachable or don't know what they're doing? I know that I knew what I was doing. What I didn't know and still don't know is how to do otherwise. How can anyone create a life that isn't one big misunderstanding? Laura Laura Laura, if I can't look at you, how will I know I exist? That was what happened there, in the toilet, when you looked at me. No one had looked at me before. Not like you did, Laura. And all those years I tormented myself and did everything wrong, what I wanted was just for you to go on looking at me so I could know I existed, that I had a body and I could live. I'm not asking you to kill me because I don't love you. I know you could go to jail for that, in all these years I watched the news and all the documentaries on TV, and I'm not that woman cut off from the world anymore. I even subscribed to the newspaper and always read your magazine. And when you sort through the apartment to sell it, you'll find all your articles in homemade albums. And I read and watched all the books and films you referred to, secretly hoping that one day the two of us might talk about them like some mothers and daughters do. I'm only asking you to kill me because I won't be able to bear it if I can't look at you. I just need to look at you. Yours is the last image I want to take with me from life. And even though I didn't know how to love, I think that is a kind of love. Even if I didn't act as I should have, as you were right to say I should have, what I felt for you, even when I hated you, was the deepest, most complete feeling I've felt in this world and in my whole life. And I only asked you to kill me, Laura, out of love. I don't want to write any more. Words never did me any good, even though I've enjoyed writing this diary of late. But it's enough. When there are too many of them, words can be unpredictable. It's not easy to use the right words. If it was a word that killed my father, I want to choose the last word I'm going to write. Now that I can choose my words and they'll no longer rape me. I want to have the last word. And I want it to be alive, so it lives with me even in death. So I can know it makes sense, that something makes sense in the big misunderstanding that is life. So that in the midst of the horror of death, of the fear that controls me like the cat eating me from inside, I have this word to save me from total darkness. The only word I wanted to write, born of my desire. Because you weren't born as a result of your father shoving himself into my paralyzed body. You were born when you looked at me, and I saw myself in your gaze. I wanted you to live. You're the only bit of life I can feel in me now that I'm dying.

30

Laura

31

When I look at my mother in the morning, lying in the bed that's now too big for her, I almost feel sorry. She looks so vulnerable. My mother is afraid, and seeing her so fearful doesn't give me the pleasure I thought it would. I can see tiny green dots in her brown eyes. Now they contrast with the lethal yellow of the disease. Mom, did you know your eyes are sort of green? She looks at me blankly. Were the green dots always there, and I just never noticed? I'm in pain, Laura. Give me the medicine. I hand my mother four red tablets and she swallows them without water. Luckily, there are plenty of painkillers in the bedside table. I think of that word dumbwaiter, presumably a remnant from more aristocratic times, a word I'd always thought so cruel. I'd been a kind of dumbdaughter myself, about as eloquent as that piece of furniture. Those painkillers aren't going to keep my mother's pain at bay much longer. I'd better take her to the hospital soon so they can start getting her ready for surgery. I'm not so bad, after all.

Mom, I've thought about it carefully, and I can't kill you. First, it's illegal. I'd be sent to jail. I know you don't care if I go to jail, but I'd rather not go. You know, the food in there isn't great. And you wouldn't be around to bring me cigarettes. Second, I wouldn't be able to kill you. Even though that option used to appeal to me, I'm not a murderer. So, this is what we're going to do, Mommie Dearest. Yes, she's my Joan Crawford. You have to go back to the hospital and undergo treatment. That's it. No one wants to get sick, but it happens. You have to see that, until now, you've been as healthy as a horse. You've lived well all these years and now you need to face up to cancer. I'm going to be at your side, don't worry.

I don't want to go, Laura. You know what they want to do to me and you know it's not worth it. Call me a coward, if you like, but I don't want to suffer more than I already am. Let me die at home, please. Pass me that load of painkillers and I'll kill myself.

My mother is begging, and I want to scream that this woman isn't my mother, my mother never begged for anything or asked for mercy. I feel angry because she's letting me down at the end of her life. I can't, Mom. I just can't. What kind of daughter would I be if I left you helpless? No, no, I'll do everything for you. My mother could write a book called Daughter Dearest, if she lives long enough, that is.

At that moment I feel so powerful. And cruel. I want to hurt her because she's abandoning me. All of a sudden I understand that my mother is going to leave me. That I won't have a mother to hate anymore. As bad as she's been, she was the only one who stayed. And in her own warped way, she was there, if only to make my days miserable. It's not a game between the two of us anymore. Death puts an end to all games.

I want to kill her by tearing off chunks of her flesh with my fingernails. Not out of hate, but out of love. Out of desperation. Because she's going to leave me. And I'll be the only one left. A body dragging a corpse.

Mom, I can't. I'm going to call the hospital.

I call the psychologist's direct number, because I've always had her in the palm of my hand and she thinks highly of me. I explain that I lost courage, out of love, only ever out of love, and I did what my mother wanted, but I can't go through with it, she needs the best help and we can pay for private treatment. In the wing that doesn't have peeling paint and doesn't smell of disinfectant. Or of cheap scent, which is a shame. Yes, we have the means to pass through the door between two worlds. She explains that in the private wing there's another psychology team, and I can feel the resentment in her voice. But she'll talk to her colleague there, of course, and explain the case. I thank her effusively and start packing a bag for my mother. My mother's funny. I discover that she has a drawer containing nothing but pajamas and nightdresses for the hospital. In some way, she's prepared herself for this day. She wants to die with the smell of her life. The question is whether the soap will stand this final test. Now I can make out the smell of death on my mother's skin. The smell of old woman and disease. The smell of a body that's decaying while the heart is still beating, more out of habit, because it was programmed to pump blood until it breaks. I slyly sniff my arm. I'm starting to decompose too. I can smell it. I'm just a few steps behind, that's all. But my body started dying years ago. The world is a field of zombies. Like brilliant yellow sunflowers that next week will be black. I saw a field of black sunflowers once. I think it was the saddest thing I've ever seen.

My mother isn't talking to me anymore. She's not mute, she's panicking. The disease has left her prostrate, not even her nails seem threatening anymore, they're just brittle. I have the same crumbling nails on my hands, but mine are still young. I realize I could do anything to her, and that scares me. Let's go, Mom. The hospital is ready to readmit you, and it's better to get it over and done with. Come on, I'll help you get up. I already called a taxi.

My mother looks around her. She knows she won't see her apartment again. Her home. She knows a whole life will survive her, only to disappear. The furniture and the objects that have meaning for her alone will be sold or given away, and there'll be nothing of her left in the world. Except for me, and I'm trying to get her out of me with a knife.

I can read all of this in her yellow eyes with green dots, and I feel tears welling up in my own. Come on, Mom, you might still come back. They're just things, they don't mean anything. What I'm saying is horrible, I know that. They're not things, they're her life. When she stops breathing, it'll be like magic in reverse. But that won't make sense for anyone who's left, not even me. First the body, then the memory. Finally, a smudge. Eventually, not even the smudge. In her gaze, I can make out the horror of someone leaving her home to die in the aseptic atmosphere of a hospital. Leaving home is simply the first departure with no return. Saying goodbye to the apartment in the knowledge that she won't come back. No, I can't grasp it.

I'm sorry, Mom, I say. I'm sorry, but I can't do any better than this. I discover that it's true, that in my twisted way I am doing my best. Her expression changes. I think she understands. She doesn't look back when the apartment door closes and she rides the elevator down for the last time. And she pretends not to see the old people on the bench or the women with their dogs. And the dog doesn't even stop shitting for that moment. In the end, that's life. Only when dying do we discover that there's grandeur in the scenes that make up these pathetic days. And that there's poetry in a dog shitting.

I can feel what she's feeling. And right now, I want to die with my mother. Because the days to come won't make any sense without her. I won't be able to see them clearly without her. And even now, when I'm protecting her, when I'm almost carrying her, I know she's the one protecting and carrying me. That we only know how to walk together. And that, without her, I'll have no legs.

The staff waiting for us at the hospital are visibly annoyed by our escape. When they see us, however, something in those white-coated characters breaks. Because our truth is so painful that it reaches the lobby before we do. And what they see is a daughter and mother in death's antechamber who have just discovered that everything was one big misunderstanding. And now their time is up.

When my mother is settled into bed and the nurses start taking samples for the tests they'll do before the operation, I realize I can't take it anymore. I've reached my limit. I flee like the most despicable daughter.

Mom, I have to go to the bookstore. Today is Wednesday.

Wednesday? she stammers, confused.

Yes, on Wednesdays I go to the bookstore.

I slam the door and run down the corridor. Four blocks away, I realize I'm still running.

32

There he is. This time he's holding the last Harry Potter book. Why the last one? I can't forgive J. K. Rowling for having killed Harry Potter, I say in greeting. A kind smile spreads across his face. He has really white teeth. Does he get them whitened? He doesn't look like the kind of person to get his teeth whitened. I notice that his bottom teeth are like cat's teeth. Small and pointy. But I'm not afraid of his teeth. My mother is dying, I say. And I throw my arms around him in the middle of the bookstore, in the self-help section. How ironic, I think, it's like a bad film script. I cry like a child. Scandalously, convulsively. He holds me, and his nice hands shelter me. He doesn't say anything while I sob and soak his shirt with snot and tears. I want to spend my life inside him, into your arms, like that song says. I realize that this near stranger, whose name I don't even know, the Harry Potter man, is the person closest to me. When I finally stop crying, a million years later, I feel ashamed. People nearby shoot sidelong glances at me, some of them offended by my public demonstration of animal pain. Others delight in my suffering. Here's a story to tell at home, to inject a bit of emotion into your plain lives, I curse. Shhhhhh, he says. And hugs me again, as if I'm a little girl. And in some way that's what I am. A daughter.

Let's get out of here, he says. And I grab his hand and follow, pleased that someone knows where to go and what to do. He explains that his clinic is nearby. And when I wake from my torpor, we're already in an elevator. The operator talks to the Harry Potter man about the final of the Brazilian championship and doesn't seem fazed by a woman with red hair, a puffy face, and broken nails. We stop on the first floor, and he opens the door to a room where I immediately feel good. The sun comes in through gaps in the curtain just enough not to need the light on, and there's a smell of peppermint in the air. I feel like I'm in a cup of tea. Take your clothes off. I don't think I want to have sex right now, I say. We're not going to have sex. I'm going to give you a massage. Some affection. I don't know if I'll like it, but I do what he says.

When I lie on the Indian rug on the floor, I feel scared. I don't like receiving anything. I never turn my back to anyone, I say. I try to flip him over so he's pinned underneath me. I want to eat you up. I want your dick deep inside me and I want to pull the head of your dick off. No, this isn't sex, he protests softly, and I can see he's trying to stifle a laugh. Maybe later, maybe one day. For now, you need a massage. Trust me, you're going to like it. I don't trust him. But I don't have the energy to put up a fight anymore. I don't want to get up from there. If I leave that room, I'll have to go back to the hospital. Let him do what he wants with me. I don't mind being raped so long as I can stay lying down, smelling the peppermint in the air.

It feels so good to have his hands on me. His fingers follow the intricate web of small scars that cover my body and he doesn't ask any questions. My scars are like a subway map, I think. He strums my marks and I can almost hear the music. I remember a story I once read. A Chinese girl lives alone in a hospital bed. One day a fly flutters its wings against her face. It's the first time in her whole life that she's felt a caress. Every morning from that day on, the fly's wings stroke her face and bring her unexpected happiness. The fly's wings cure the girl. But I think I'm making up the end. In the story, the fly gets squashed, and the girl dies. It doesn't matter. I could die here. And I think I'd almost be happy.

I feel, more than hear, a noise my spine makes. A click. And I want to cry. I'm melting, I say to him. And he says. It's all right. And it is. Now the current of my tears is slower, a placid stream between rounded stones. I think I'm crying for the width and breadth of an existence. But maybe that's just a feeling. While his hands are still on me, everything is all right. His hands provide borders for the territory of my body. You gave me a body, I say. No, he smiles. I'm just reminding you that it's yours. And that it doesn't always hurt.

I'm impaled by the thought. All my muscles tense up again, and adrenaline shoots through me like liquid ice. He says, Calm down, calm down, relax. No, I can't relax anymore. I need to run. I almost knock him over when I get up and start putting on my clothes, getting the buttons in the wrong holes. What happened? he says. I can feel the frustration in his voice. It's not because of you, you have to understand that. Or maybe it is because of you, actually. I need to kill my mother.

He looks at me in shock. For the first time something I say shocks the Harry Potter man, the dear Harry Potter man. I can't leave my mother to suffer, you have to understand that. I have to do this for her. For me too, I think. I have to run. Now he's frozen, but I know he's not going to turn me in.

Do you know how I can kill my mother?

He doesn't answer. And I know it's not right to bring him into this. And I want to do the right thing. I slam the door. Then I open it again.

Please, wait for me next Wednesday.

33

How can someone kill her own mother?

It's not a moral question for me. It's a practical one. While the taxi takes me to the hospital, I try to remember everything I've read about suicide and euthanasia. Cocaine overdose? It wouldn't be hard to get some coke, just a couple of phone calls. But it doesn't strike me as a painless death, and the doctors might detect the drug. It would be more efficient to do it with something routinely used in the hospital. What do they put in lethal injections on death row? Potassium chloride, I read that once. But where am I going to get hold of that? They must keep that kind of stuff locked away, although it's always possible to convince someone. Bribe a nursing assistant, maybe. They're always poorly paid. And they're the ones with the best idea of how each ward works, they're there twenty-four hours a day, getting their hands dirty so the doctors and even the nurses can keep theirs clean. The problem is that a crime involving more than one person is no longer perfect.

I ask the taxi driver to make a detour and stop in front of my bank. I explain to the bank manager that my mother needs emergency surgery, and I need money, cash, to make some arrangements. He argues that it's difficult to get hold of such a large amount at such short notice, but my expression remains firm. I'm not going to leave there without my money. I don't argue, I just stare at the manager and wait. And he finds a way in the end. I leave the bank with a wad of notes fat enough to buy an accomplice.

When I return to my mother's room, the black-feathered-doctor is there. I'm jumpy and I'd rather my mother was alone. I didn't know you'd carry on looking after my mother, I say. In fact, I wouldn't normally be here. But I care about your mother and I'm going to assist the team. The doctor seems less fragile today. Perhaps because I feel weak and, I realize this now, almost panicked by what I'm about to do. I have to keep control of myself, I absolutely have to. Oh, great, I say. It's wonderful to have such a dedicated professional looking after my mother. I'm not even sure if I'm being ironic or not. She doesn't seem to mind, anyway. It's good that you're here. This way, I can explain to you both what the next steps will be. We'll operate the day after tomorrow. We've already done all the necessary tests. It seems there's nothing to prevent us carrying out the procedure. Because you're in a lot of pain, Maria Lúcia, we're going to start using morphine to make you more comfortable. There's nothing to worry about. People often get scared when we mention morphine, but there's nothing to worry about. Morphine is an excellent medication, it's very efficient and the body tolerates it well. A nurse will be along soon to give you your daily dose. We'll start with a high dose, given your condition, but you'll get it gradually, diluted in a drip. You'll feel the difference right away. You might even feel like eating something tasty that your daughter could bring for you. The doctor looks at me and smiles. I return the closest thing to a smile I can manage.

In fact, I want to give the long-legged-doctor a kiss. Now the crime is mine alone. Thank you, doctor. We're very grateful for your help. She looks at me in surprise when she senses my sincerity. You idiot, I say to myself, you have to carry on being as much of a bitch as ever if you don't want to draw attention to yourself. You can do better than that. I get ready to say something unpleasant, but the doctor is already at the door, promising to come back the next day.

I take my mother's hands, which are increasingly different from my own now that the disease is molding her in its image and likeness. Cancer is like being possessed by an alien from the inside out. The cancer that's mutilating her is as much part of my mother as the healthy cells failing to defend her from their sisters. It's a horror movie, filmed from the inside. Science fiction that isn't fiction. I'm fascinated by everyday life's capacity for horror. Why invent zombies and aliens from outer space when we have cancer?

I'm going to kill you, Mom. At first she looks at me in surprise, then with cautious hope. How are you going to do it, Laura? I don't want you to get locked up on my behalf. I think I was being selfish. I squeeze her fingers, and she moans. Don't worry, leave it all to me. I know what to do. You're going to die painlessly, I promise. And with your body intact. And when, Laura? When am I going to die? Sometime tonight, Mom. Before tomorrow comes.

I see her yellow and green eyes fill with tears. Laura, I'm scared of dying. I don't want to leave you. You know, I think I've discovered now that I like living. Isn't that ironic? And my mother starts laughing, a laugh that comes slowly, in chapters. Tears run down my face as well. I'll miss you, Mom. But I'll be here. I'll be with you until the end. She cries quietly. And I rest my head against hers. We stay like that until the nurse comes to inject the morphine into the drip. I catch her wiping away a tear when she sees us.

When the nurse leaves, I ask my mother if she wants to eat anything special, anything at all. She says she's not hungry, the toxins given out by her tumors are poisoning her blood. Is there anything you want, Mom? Are you asking me if I have a last wish, Laura? Like someone on death row? No, Mom, because they don't get to choose when they die. And you've chosen, Mom. Just the date, Laura. I only brought the date forward. In some way, we're all condemned to death, aren't we? Even that puffed-up doctor who thinks he's going to operate on me. I see now that the moment always comes when we can no longer choose to live, the best we can do is choose how to die.

My mother doesn't seem like my mother. Why isn't she staying silent as usual? Sorry, Laura. I wish I'd chosen life when it was still possible. You did choose, Mom. Even without knowing, you chose it. And you lived. And you're going to live. It's not over yet.

I touch her hand. And she grabs me with strength she shouldn't have anymore. Laura, there is one thing I want before I die. Go on, Mom, anything. I want to watch The Sound of Music.

It takes me a while to understand, for the image of Julie Andrews twirling about the Austrian mountains to come to mind. Without sound. No sound at all. Julie Andrews is moving her mouth, but I can't hear her. But, Mom, you hate that movie. I know, but I need to see it.

I slam the hospital door for the second time. This reality is too much, each of my steps feels heavy as if I'm walking on the ocean floor. I'm going to fall into the abyss inhabited by blind fish. But I don't fall. I'm just pretending to inhabit

Laura's body. I'm someone else. I'm the Silver Surfer watching Earth from his surfboard, moved by human drama. It's the best film ever, the girl in the video store says with a smile. I've seen it eight times. Do you want popcorn to go with it? We've got brownies too.

Do I want popcorn? Mom, do you want popcorn before you die?

34

It took me no more than thirty minutes, but when I get back to my mother's room, night has fallen. And at night, all the wild beasts escape from inside us and bare their teeth, and we hide them in flannel pajamas so no one finds us out. Today, however, I'm supposedly the monster threatening the world's machine. And the pitch-dark serves to conceal the crime of helping my mother to die. I'm aided by the reduced number of nursing assistants, people feigning sleep in other rooms, the dimmed lights in the corridor, and the respectful fear that darkness has imposed since ancient times—times that still breathe within us.

Now that my mother's life is coming to an end, everything seems so incredibly solemn. I realize that my mother experienced her last sunset. And now there'll be only night for her. Just one night. If she's lucky, I'll manage to kill her before dawn. Kill her to save her, logic subverts itself. I never imagined that everything I desired out of hate would, in the end, be an act of love.

I got the film, Mom. Aren't these luxury wards with cable TV and DVD players amazing? She doesn't seem amazed. I want to say stupid, facile things. I'm desperate for a hint of normality amidst the horror of this scene in which we play the lead roles, the secret burning between us like one of those children's birthday candles that never goes out. Blow it out and it flickers back up. Blow it out and it flickers back up. Trample on it.

My heart is beating so hard that the skin over my chest hurts. And I think I can hear my mother's heartbeat. Du-dum, Du-dum, Du-dum. The girl at the video store asked if I wanted popcorn, can you imagine? And I laugh a laugh that isn't mine. My mother doesn't laugh. It's like she isn't even there.

I put the movie in the machine. I get mixed up with the buttons. I'm lousy with remote controls, all of them. My mother's the one who could always understand gadgets, even the most modern ones. Where's play? Maybe my mother would like to press rewind? Which chapter would she go back to? Mom, do you want to take the remote? I ask. My mother looks at me, and I know what she's thinking. No, Laura, you keep it. I just want to watch the film.

Now I can hear the music. But it's still quieter than the sound of my heartbeat. When should I start killing her? It's like pulling a trigger. She's my mother. Yes, you idiot. It's because she's your mother that you have to pluck up the courage to help her die. I can't do it. You can, you promised her. It's her best chance. If you don't do it right, you'll have to smother her with a pillow, like in the movies. And that's why you have to get up from the chair now and walk to the drip as if to check that it's working. Then, you just make the movement.

There are two voices inside me. I have to split myself in two to bear it. I get up quickly. But it's just an illusion. Only my legs moved, kicking the bed and making a metallic sound. Sorry, Mom. She doesn't respond. I turn to see her face and find a childish expression. My mother is entranced by the movie. What happened to her? She always hated this movie, especially because I loved it. Well, think what's going on, you idiot. She's dying. Death changes your perspective on things. Or at least I think it does. I can't take my eyes off her face. She seems not to notice my presence. She isn't even there. My mother is walking over the green mountains around Salzburg. Or she's pretending to. She's pretending so hard, she believes it.

I get up, softly now, and I stoop as I pass in front of the television. She doesn't seem to notice. I move the drip slightly. I make believe. On the screen, Julie Andrews is singing The Sound of Music. It's my favorite part of the movie. The beginning. Julie Andrews has her arms wide open, and she's spinning.

I release the mechanism, and now the drip runs quickly. It's done. Can my mother hear the mountains' song? Is my mother's heart singing for the last time? Did my mother's heart ever sing?

All I need is for a nursing assistant to come in now and it'll all be fine. I lean against the wall. My mother can't see me. Cold sweat soaks my hair and runs down my legs. I'm melting. No, I'm not. I'm whole. It's done. I notice, for the first time, that Julie Andrews seems to have too many teeth. I'm afraid of Julie Andrews' mouth full of teeth. Why doesn't she stop singing?

I look at my mother out of the corner of my eye as I sit down again. She simply blinks. A stronger blink. She knows. Thank you, Mom, for not saying anything. I take her hand. I want to feel close, but I can't do it. My hand is on hers, but light-years away. I breathe in the smell of her hand. I smile. She managed to wash her hands with her soap before dying. That's typical of my mother. Now I feel close. Watch the movie, Laura. Just watch the movie. Yes, Mom. A gentle knock, and the door opens. I clamp my heart between molars and canines. It's a nursing assistant. Please don't come in, for the love of God, don't come in. My mother looks at her with a smile I've never seen before. We're watching The Sound of Music. Can you come back later? I love this film. I'm so happy!

The girl pauses at the door. It's a joke how thin she is, and the huge bags under her eyes make her look older. She must work in two different hospitals to earn a bit more, must leave one shift to start another. I want to say something, but I can't. If I try, I know my heart will leap onto the floor and I'll turn into the Tin Man. She gives a tired smile. I'll come back when the movie ends. If you need anything, just press the button next to the bed. Of course, thank you, dear, says my mother with another beatific smile.

I'm in a state of shock. My mother could win an Oscar for that performance. I look at her out of the corner of my eye, but she just seems absorbed in the movie. Thank you, Mom. I think I need to tell her I love her and I know I need to hurry up, but I don't know how to do it. I take her hand again. She looks at me. Laura, I know. Now, watch the movie. Father Von Trapp is going home, he doesn't know yet that he's going to fall for the rebellious governess. Laura. I shudder when I hear my mother's voice. Do you think that, when he died, Churchill knew his life had been worthwhile?

What is she talking about? Mom, I didn't think you even knew who Churchill was. I was just thinking, Laura. But we'd better carry on watching the movie. Father von Trapp is in love now but he's fighting his own feelings, and Maria needs to leave. I hear a soft noise. My mother's breathing

seems shallower. I want to shout. Mom, wait, Maria is going
to come back and everything will be OK! There's no sound,
in the real scene I'm an actress in a silent movie. Maria,
don't leave me! I'm the children in the movie. Or am I me?
I take my mother's hand and stare at the screen, but I can't
see anything anymore.

When I'm back in my skin. Or when I seem to be back,
the final credits are rolling up the screen. I'm afraid to look.
But the hand underneath mine, my hand, has already left
me alone. My mother looks like she's sleeping. That's a lie.
She looks like she's dead. The dead look like they're dead.
No, Mom! I shout now. I really shout. But it's too late. It was
always too late. I grab the bell and press the button hard.
The thin nursing assistant moves me aside incredibly gently.

I hug myself and cry, curled up like the woodlouse from
my childhood. I'm a picture of loneliness and helplessness
in the hospital room. A grown woman in a fetal position
when the woman who brought her into the world has just
left it. She took her womb with her.

35

The nursing assistant checks the drip. I don't care anymore. I'm not afraid. I'm beyond that. She seemed so well, she was even talking to me a little while ago. The thin girl is talking more to herself than to anyone else. Now she knows. My future depends on that small woman with eyes aged by so much death. I don't pay much attention. The assistant takes my hands, which aren't like anyone's in the world anymore, and says, It's better this way. Your mother didn't suffer. She died in her sleep at a nice moment. Her heart simply stopped. Sometimes that happens to patients. It's god who decides when we die. No, it's not god, I want to say. But I just nod my head.

The thin girl made a choice, and I hug her tightly. Thank you. She pretends not to understand. You don't need to thank me, I didn't even have time to care for your mother. She was hardly here with us. The doctors won't come to write the death certificate until tomorrow. Today the staff are all stressed out, you know what hospitals are like, the emergency room always overflowing. In the meantime, let's get your mother ready. Is there anyone who can help you with the arrangements? No, there isn't. How am I managing to speak? I'm amazed that I can speak and move. But I can. My mother is going to be cremated. That was what she wanted. It's what I have to do. No trace. A long day's journey into night. Incinerated.

When the edge of morning starts to lift, and I'm surprised that the sun rises in a world without my mother, the black-feathered-doctor arrives. She has her doubts, I know. She's going to need plenty of extra feathers now. But the thin girl is emphatic as she explains how my mother was happily watching the movie. It's good that she died in her sleep, painlessly, isn't it, doctor? She looks at me with her caged bird's eyes. I say, Thank you for everything you've done for us. And she knows that I'm beyond fear. I wish you the best of luck with life, she says. Having a life at all is enough for me, I want to say. But I just thank her with a nod.

I wait, alone, for my mother's ashes. In a few days' time, I'll call Alzira-from-the-spiritualist-center. She might be able to find my mother when she communicates with the other side. Who knows? I know my mother is in these ashes I'm holding. But she's not, at the same time. My mother is in my body that's hers. No. It's mine. My body with memories of her. For the first time, I want my mother to be inside me. Not as a possession, I understand now. But as a memory.

The taxi driver wants to talk, I can tell. He glances uncomfortably at the urn in my hand. I pretend not to notice. He can't bear it. To me, cremation just doesn't seem right. What if the person needs their body where they've gone?

If she needs a body, she'll come and get mine.

36

She sits on the bench in the apartment building's garden. Her powdered mother in her lap. She's surprised how she always sticks with the lie of light. Hidden in the sun, she and her hell. Like the little old man who's making a vague gesture on the other bench. And the women with the shitting dogs. And the doorman who's looking at her but pretending he's not, his bloodless tongue lolling out. It's another normal day. And she's no more or less normal than everyone else. She knows that now. That's their secret. Hers too, now that she knows how to camouflage herself in the light.

She follows the path of a thin scar that disappears up her shirtsleeve. She knows the whole map of cuts that makes her body hers. The geography forged by her penknife. It makes no difference, she realizes now. The uncut flesh is also hers. And do her mother's ashes in her lap still contain her mother's flesh? Is that what a body is, in the end?

He hair shines in the sun. The bright blood that doesn't run off. If the light weren't so deceptive, she would be able to make out the strand there in the middle. White. Her body outlived her mother's, imposed itself on time. She doesn't know. Not yet, not at that moment. But her body is betraying her by the second. And with time, instead of fire, she'll be snow. Yes,

Laura, her mother's voice seems to whisper. You started dying before you'd even said a word. You were already dying, Laura, before the word.

No life is ever complete. She knows that now. Like her mother, she too will wait for something to be complete, but her life will carry on to an open, inconclusive end. Human life is the only life that finishes without an end, because it's the only life that expects one. She opens the lid of the urn and pushes her right hand inside. She wants to feel the texture of her mother. But her mother's body remains intangible.

She needs to go up to the apartment, but she doesn't have the strength. Not yet. She's especially scared of the shoes. Shoes are the worst, she thinks. Almost indecent in their abandonment, their marks. Steps, falls, sprains, stumbles, kinks in the spine. It's all there. Dead people's shoes should be censored for their shamelessness. No, she doesn't have the strength to face the shoes. She doesn't have the courage to face her mother's world without her mother.

She gets up and walks away from the building. She walks quickly to the video store. The smiling, talkative girl is there. Did you like the movie? Isn't it the most beautiful movie you've seen in your life? Yes, she says. It's lovely.

She knows now that she's going to survive. Life is only possible on the surface. Have a nice week, says the girl. You too.

37

I'm exhausted. Writing fiction is like lending my body to myself.

I wrote so I could kill my mother. This is the only possibility literature has to offer. And maybe so I could love her.

This knife doesn't hurt any less when it cuts my body off. And like writing on the computer, there's no blood or matter. The insanity of this body that can't be touched confuses me. I discover that I wrote about the impossibility of literature. The failure that I'd previously assumed in trying to turn life into words. The most important thing is what can't be written, what screams formlessly and voicelessly between the lines. What can never be said. It's better that way, let it be that way.

The Harry Potter man asks me:

"This book you wrote, is it like a child?"

"Yes and no. A novel is always a child. But a child from hell. And it is legion."

About the Author

Eliane Brum was born in 1966 in the southern Brazilian city of Ijuí. She has worked as a journalist, writer, and documentary filmmaker. In more than two decades of reporting she has won over forty national and international awards in journalism, among them the Premio Rey de España and the Inter-American Associated Press Award. In 2008, she received the United Nations Special Press Trophy. She also codirected and cowrote the 2005 documentary film *Uma história severina (Severina's Story)*, winner of seventeen national and international awards. Eliane Brum currently works as a freelance journalist and writes a column for *El País*. She has published five collections of nonfiction. *One Two* is her first novel.

About the Translator

Lucy Greaves is a UK-based translator of Spanish, Portuguese, and French. She won the 2013 Harvill Secker Young Translators' Prize and was Translator in Residence at London's Free Word Centre during 2014.